7509 81

P9-ELT-090

WITHDRAWN

ALSO BY

FELICITY CASTAGNA

The Incredible Here and Now
Small Indiscretions

NO MORE BOATS

Felicity Castagna

NO MORE BOATS

Europa
editions

Europa Editions
214 West 29th Street
New York, N.Y. 10001
www.europaeditions.com
info@europaeditions.com

This book is a work of fiction. Any references to historical events,
real people, or real locales are used fictitiously.

Copyright © 2017 by Felicity Castagna
First publication: 2017 by Giramondo Publishing
First US publication: 2019 by Europa Editions

Library of Congress Cataloging in Publication Data is available
ISBN 978-1-60945-509-5

Castagna, Felicity
No More Boats

Book design by Emanuele Ragnisco
www.mekkanografici.com

Cover photo © Paola Quintavalle

Prepress by Grafica Punto Print – Rome

Printed in the USA

For my father, who came here on a boat

'For those who've come across the seas
we've boundless plains to share;
with courage let us all combine
to advance Australia fair'

NO MORE BOATS

Before

I t is 1967. The Australian Prime Minister, Mr. Harold Holt, swims out into the ocean and gets eaten by a shark. Or he gets picked up by a Chinese submarine and becomes a spy. It's possible that he just shouldn't be swimming, despite his reputation as a sportsman, because he's thrown his shoulder out of alignment and is taking morphine and also because he might be depressed and maybe he doesn't want to live anymore. Others say he is murdered because he opposes building military bases at Pine Gap, or because he relaxed the White Australia Policy so that the Asians can invade.

It could also be because the oceans around Australia are rough places where boats are known to fall apart and people get caught in rips they can't see and the people and the boats just disappear and no one knows why, or sometimes they do know, but no one wants to talk about what really happens out there. Not *really*, anyway.

It is the day after Harold Holt has disappeared and Antonio Martone is standing in his new home. He is not yet *the* Antonio Martone who becomes so famous for a brief moment in history when his own existential crisis coincides with that of a nation that can't decide whether to let in a Norwegian container ship named the MV *Tampa* and its cargo of 438 human beings, who'd almost disappeared into the ocean, like Harold Holt. For that brief moment between the unwanted ship sitting out there off the coast and the planes colliding into twin towers in another country, Antonio is everywhere holding that gun that may or may not have been his. He's staring blankly out of everyone's television sets and out of the copies of the *Daily Telegraph* you always find discarded next to you on the train seat.

For now though, he is just Antonio and he's standing here thinking about how the future has finally picked its way out of his head and materialised in front of him. He lays his body down in the middle of the living room and thinks about what he has built. He always knew that the future was waiting for him in this new land across the sea. White aluminium siding, aluminium eight-over-eights, yellow fibreboard shutters, high rectangular windows, crisp brown linoleum marking the path to the kitchen. Upstairs there are three bedrooms, two baths: total square footage, twelve hundred and sixty-five. He's done the front door in an arch. People don't always understand how much harder it is to bend wood and concrete into a half-moon shape than it is to leave it in straight angular lines, but he knows; it is a deep and private satisfaction to him every time he walks through his own front door.

His house is on a one-acre block, big enough for a market garden out the back. He will grow olives and bergamots like his father did. This is what he has dragged out of the raw earth that had been here, just a big dry tangle of a paddock on the only hill in town—a place of small brown nondescript birds. The house is east-facing. His wife's body casts a long shadow over him as she walks through the door.

'Antonio,' Rose says, looking at him lying there on the floor, 'I think you love this house more than me.'

She walks towards him, bringing her soapy smell; the soft clicking of herself. She rubs her belly, hoping she will be pregnant soon. If it is a girl they will name her Clare; if it is a boy, Francis. They walk together through the house and into the front yard where he has recently laid another slab of concrete.

'Not much room to build a flower bed,' Rose says.

'Later. I make different.' But he knows he won't. It is cleaner this way. It makes the land look more solid. His wife wants so many impractical things. He locks the door and puts the key on its blue piece of yarn around his neck. They turn and face the horizon where the land is being cut up and divided and cut up and divided again into finite squares. Antonio has built on the hilly east side, the only place in Parramatta that isn't flat. From this one hill it is possible to see everything: those tight brick rectangles of government housing, the fibro cottages, the old colonials, the wide stretches of nothing space in between everything. The corkscrews of smoke rise out of the factories in Silverwater and Granville to the east. There is the rumble of roads being poured, of concrete and bitumen stretching out towards his house to take it in. In the distance the sound of railway lines screeching and moving closer.

Antonio looks towards the river but he can't see it behind the mangroves. He is thinking of the point where the salt water meets fresh. He will take his line and hook out there later, to see if he can catch a fish with the other men who sit by the pier. All he wants is this, his own patch of land, this moment in the afternoon; the future to keep coming and coming.

1

On the TV talk of inundation and floods, rising tides, tsunamis of human beings coming across the ocean, all headed here. A watery invasion threatening to drag us under. Too many boats. Same thing they've been anxious about since yesterday, the day before that, two hundred years ago.

And at this moment, 31 August 2001, a day on which the Parramatta River was overflowing down near the Ferry Pier, where this story begins and ends, there was flooding too. The footpaths around the river's edge were underwater. Disgruntled teenagers drank on the top of the grassy slopes because their usual spot on the benches below had become submerged. The old Chinese women with their Mandarin-playing boomboxes must have been doing their nightly riverside aerobics somewhere else, the Lebanese men had stopped fishing near the housing commission flats and got their fish at the markets instead. The tradies at the Workers Club pressed cold beers to their mouths and smoked their ciggies on the balcony and made jokes about how the river could swallow their utes in the parking lot while the public servants from the newly relocated offices of Sydney Water and Electricity stared out towards the river behind the polished windows of their bloated office blocks.

Antonio's son Francis stood on the riverbank and looked out to the mangroves at the ferry that was making its way to the slim top of the pier that hadn't been swallowed by the water and said 'fuck' into the evening air. He had just shoved his hands into his saggy jeans and discovered that he was out of cigarettes. He backtracked slightly down the road behind the river and went to the corner store he had been avoiding on account of the man working there being an old friend of his father's who was going to ask him, for sure, about what his father had done.

Do you know what his father did?

Of course you do.

Everyone wanted to know about it but what the fuck did Francis know?

When Francis entered the shop Ron said, 'Yer fa-dah, hah!'

Francis shrugged his shoulders and put his money on the counter and pissed off out of there as soon as the cigarettes were in his hand. No explanation. He wasn't trying to explain it to anyone. He hardly understood it himself.

Back on his way. He walked down the street, just puffin'. The man with no left arm stood there by his letterbox like usual, watching the road. Francis kicked a rock as he passed him. He pretended to be interested in the rock and all, so he didn't have to look the man in the face. It was the same street he'd walked down on the way to Charbel's place since they were in primary school. There were the same old Eels banners hanging slack from the fibro cottages since their last win, same old convict graveyards, same people floating down the street like they were cruising even when they were not in their cars, the same women in hot pink Spandex running towards the river.

Dawn of a new century, 2001 and all that, but things were pretty much the same as they were in high school except now Francis was five years older and he spent his days laying bricks instead of waiting outside the principal's office. His two best mates were still Jesús and Charbel. On weekends there was still nothing to do. Women weren't really interested in

Charbel and Francis but they were interested in Jesús. Jesús could put it on like he was one of those Latino playboys from the *telenovelas* his mother watched. He even did the slicked-back hair and the patent leather shoes and the walking up to a girl at The Albion like he was dancing a salsa or some shit like that. But that wasn't really who he was. Francis would've acted like that too if he'd thought it might've helped him get laid. When Jesús wasn't with a girl, Francis and Charbel hung out at his place. Charbel was still boring. Francis was still angry with his father for lots of things like being crazy and stubborn and unable to take him seriously, but mostly, at this moment, for giving him a pussy name like Francis.

He walked. The sun set through the spaces between the buildings and spread itself across the road like a kind of golden slime. There was a mania for sitting on plastic chairs on the lawn outside the apartment blocks. People just stewing. Cigarettes in hand. The local newspapers on the ground everywhere. Someone had drawn a red line underneath the headline in the *Parramatta Sun*: ' It's Not Racist if They Come Without Their Visas!'

And then he was back down by the river again where people had gathered on the grass to point at the things being swallowed by the water. Summer was on its way and even this early, before things got really hot, the place was on heat. Walking past The Albion he could see the women were already out in their short shorts and high heels, standing in the courtyard. A blonde woman in tight white jeans leant against the brick wall outside and watched the men playing footy in the park across the road.

He headed straight across the highway. Stopped to have a fantasy or two in front of the BMW SUV and the Mercedes with the convertible roof in the second-hand car yard. Jesús was mowing the lawn in front of his mother's pale blue fibro. Francis was sure that the mowing was just an excuse to take his shirt off. Jesús was the one with all the muscles, even though it was Francis and Charbel that worked with their bodies. No one would guess that of the three of them, it was Jesús who was training to be an accountant.

Jesús didn't say anything. He waved. Francis walked himself straight into the living room where Jesús' mother was dressed in her orderly's scrubs. She was leaning against the kitchen cupboard eating toast, flicking through the newspaper. Something Spanish played on the radio, and on the TV it was the five o'clock news. The kettle went off and she looked up at Francis as if he was making all that noise.

'Be good,' she said like she'd been saying since they were in primary.

The boys from school had been spending their evenings here since forever, on account of Mrs. Consalvo working nights. Even now that Charbel had his own place in one of the slicked-up new apartments just off Church Street, they still came here. Force of habit. Mrs. Consalvo must have known what went on under her small roof, but she never said anything but *you boys be good*, or *there's leftover chicken in the fridge*. She was cool like that. They called her Mami like Jesús did. All the boys called Jesús Jesus, like Jesus Christ, even though he was always telling them to say it the Spanish way, like *Hey-Seuss.*

At least Francis wasn't the only one with a pussy name.

Even though it was the end of August, Jesús still had up the banner, 'Welcome to the year 2001,' nine months after the new year had come and gone, so that he could hide the hole Francis had accidentally punched into the wall when he was high. He liked Jesús' house. It was a loud space but it felt quiet. Francis' place was quiet but it felt loud. Francis lived in a much larger house but every inch of it was taken up by his father, even when his father was just sitting on the couch saying nothing, watching the telly.

'Mami!'

Charbel was entering through the door; Mrs. Consalvo was leaving for the night. Charbel walked in with a couple of six-packs so they could drink cheaply before they got to the bars. He was wearing board shorts and a wifebeater. He would change into his favourite Tsubi jeans and polo-neck shirt right before they went out. Francis would spray Lynx deodorant over the outside of his clothes.

They were all posers in their own way.

Charbel walked to the fridge, stuck the beers in and looked over the rest of its contents. He went over to the flower-covered couch where Francis was sitting, handed him a beer and sank down six inches as soon as he sat on the cushion.

'Shit,' he said as he fell backward.

'Shit,' Francis said.

Francis took long gulps of his beer. His hands trembled. He told himself it was because he masturbated too much, but he knew it was the pot: he needed to cut down (on both things really) but he just couldn't stop. He liked the way the pot gave the world a softer edge. Even the air took on the feel of cushioned fabric, as though you could just reach out and touch it and everything else, all the things that were bothering you, just sat like a quiet old man in the background.

When Jesús came into the living room he sat on the recliner without his shirt on, sipped his beer slowly, rubbed his belly. Charbel opened another beer he'd had waiting by his feet. The nights always started out like this. Slowly. They saved all their energy for later.

Francis tried to concentrate on the TV. On the news there was a big ship and a big ocean. The only small things were the tiny dots of people sitting around shipping containers on the deck. Then there was John Howard and his eyebrows and he was saying, 'ordinary, average Australians,' over and over again, and it was all very serious and Francis couldn't get at the words.

'You coming back to work on Monday?' Charbel asked.

'Nah, maybe.'

Francis had definitely planned on going back but he was being a jerk.

'You take as much time as you need.'

It was exactly that kind of tone, like you're talking to someone's grandmother, that meant Francis had to be a jerk. It was like this: when Charbel said 'you take as much time as you need', that wasn't everything he was saying. There was a whole lot of backstory shoved into that sentence like helium stuck in one of those over-inflated balloons. The story played over in Francis' head in time lapse: Charbel's dad (who everyone called Fat Frank, on account of him being really skinny) was the contractor on a new set of McMansions near Macquarie Fields; Francis and Charbel were both working for Fat Frank on the site and that made Charbel act like he was also the boss of everything even though he was the boss of nothing. Francis should be grateful for the job because he was a very average bricklayer who may or may not turn up to work on time but he didn't really know how to be grateful for much. There's a whole lot more backstory here about how Fat Frank and his dad used to be business partners until Francis' dad had exploded about how shit their McMansions were and Fat Frank went on to make fuckloads of money and Francis' dad ended up without much.

Francis suspected that he got away with a lot because Fat Frank thought his family was pathetic, or because Fat Frank had some kind of guilt complex, or just wanted to get back at Francis' dad by hiring his son. Maybe all of the above. 'Your father Antonio, Antonio,' he was always muttering whenever he saw Francis on the site. Whatever it was, when Charbel told him he could 'take as much time as he needed', he said it in a tone that made Francis think that maybe it was the pathetic thing. 'I'll be back by Tuesday.'

'Everyone understands about your father.'

'Wednesday then.' No one understood about his father.

They drank more beers. Jesús took a shower and Charbel changed his clothes and Francis smothered himself in Lynx. Then the boys slipped out into the street and Jesús took what he had promised them out of his wallet. The three dots of pink paper sat there in his palm. They had the smallest set of wings on them. They said *take us, take flight*, and they did, the three of them standing there, staring at the granite statue of a pouncing lion on a neighbour's lawn.

Even though this was Parramatta, and even though it was never really quiet, tonight felt calm. No one spoke. They walked. Each street they passed had the same dull, brick rectangles of apartment blocks, and in between there were lost strips of lawn and too much concrete. They cut through the park. This was the park where they used to play footy on Fridays: Italians and Yugoslavs versus Asians—the Asians always lost. On Sundays everyone teamed up against the Islanders, but the Islanders always won. At night the park looked dark and grim, not like it did in the daytime when everyone was screaming and running. There was the noise of the trains everywhere, always pulling up and leaving again. The sounds skipped across the concrete as they turned the corner.

Now they were at Francis' old school. One of his old schools. He'd spent the last two years at Arthur Phillip instead of the local Catholic where he'd started out with Charbel and Jesús, because the fat old Brother who ran the place had had enough of Francis by the time he finished Year Ten. Public school. His father never got over it. The kids there were from a wholly different planet than the Catholic school ones. Francis thought he was a bad-arse before he wound up there but afterwards he learned to stay silent.

Just as he had done a few times in his school days, he picked up a rock and chucked it at the windows of the science lab. He chose those windows because he'd always failed science and because the safety glass in the windows always broke into patterns like spiders' webs and refused to fall out. It was a challenge: he was rising to the occasion. But the wings he took earlier had made him into some type of bird with no power to break glass.

It was a while before Francis realised he was still standing in the same place holding a rock, staring at his own reflection in the glass windows. Maybe he'd been there, yesterday, today, the day before, maybe he was back at school.

'Stay loose,' Jesús said, holding Francis' hand, but Francis could feel the blood pumping right through his arm and out to his palm. They cut through the library car park and walked out onto the main street. People thought nothing went on this far from the city, but they were wrong. Everybody came to Parramatta Friday and Saturday night. Everyone. Night-time and everyone went off. This was what defined the place these days—the constant parade. For instance, as he walked down the street there were two men with too-tight tops and too-big muscles, who took up most of the wide pavement just because they could, and girls who stood on the corner and waved to the cars as if they knew everyone. The cars cruised slow and loud down Church Street. They were hot pink Echoes and lowered Hondas with orange racing stripes. Chrome. Blue lights. Hubcaps glinting in the neon glow of the restaurants. There were calls back and forth, windows rolled down. Some fat bald head in Ray-Bans yelled 'hey ladies,' and twenty-somethings in hotpants smiled and said 'fuck you' in the most seductive of ways. Francis paid particular attention to the ladies: he would take them, any of them, anytime, anywhere, if only they would have him.

They walked up through the mall to the Burger King on the corner. Everyone started here before they went anywhere else. Jesús pointed to a spare table in the corner and put Charbel in charge of Francis. Francis watched as Charbel took out his door key and tried to scratch a line through 'Charbel + Lee' where he'd carved it into the wooden wall when he was in love with Lee Chang back in the day.

The music wrapped itself around Francis' body. Jesús showed up again with the food. Francis watched the red stream of light that followed his hand each time he put his arm into the bag and pulled out a burger. Then he was stuck to his chair chewing, chewing, chewing. The food was something musical. His throat was a flute. His body was light but he couldn't move. He looked at Charbel, who was trying to eat his entire burger in one mouthful.

Moving again. They were out in the open mall. St. John's Church was twice the size it usually was. Jesús was standing in the flowerbeds in front of the church. He was all movement and light. Francis found it difficult to keep track of where he was amongst all this moving. Now Jesús was next to the old men with worry beads sitting on the bench near the children's play equipment, and then he was next to the guy with a sign that says 'The End of the World is Coming' and a microphone, then he was hanging around the entrance to the Connection Arcade, smoking, talking shit in Spanish. Maybe he was skipping. Maybe he wasn't. The flight of his feet across concrete.

They went off again. They headed south towards the brighter lights of Church Street. The bikies had parked on the pavements again, just because they could. How do you join a bikie gang?

Francis would like to be one of them. They had a tribe. He'd like to be in a tribe. Francis thought he would like to sit up on the thick leather seat of one of their Harley-Davidsons. He didn't. The hot spice smell of cheap men's cologne. Somewhere, an apple hooka. People cram their legs up underneath too-small tables in front of the restaurants on the footpath.

The words 'One World' glowed in the distance. They headed towards them. The shops selling cheap shit. Shirts for five dollars. Jeans already ripped at the knees hung in the windows. Plastic cats with oversized heads that bounce in the sunlight. Everyone wanted something cheap. More two-dollar shops.

They were standing in line in front of One World. Francis stood up as straight as he could for the bouncers. He gave instructions to himself: *Get your ID out of your wallet. Hold it in your hand. Look them in the eye like you haven't been up to nothing. Play it cool.* The signs in front of the bar said: Sexy. Bounce. Karaoke.

Inside, the place was dark and cool. Blue lights skidded across the dance floor. The ceiling was stained by cigarette smoke, from the tradies who used to come for a beer after work, to the professionals who came here now from those corporations that had relocated from the city. In the corner, a giant screen played soccer from another country. Two thirty-ish men sat at the counter drinking beer, not talking. The DJ played Prince. Maybe it was retro night. Francis hoped it wasn't retro night. Three women, all with frizzy hair, drank Bacardi Breezers by the bar. Retro brought out women who looked like schoolteachers. They should have stayed in Burger King where Shaggy and Tupac brought out the girls in the short shorts. Almost ten, and there was the slow creep of people entering the place. Things began to slow again. The boys sat down at a booth in the corner. Francis lit a cigarette and watched the smoke disappear into the air in front of him.

Francis watched Jesús' eyes dart around the place. It was too loud to really hear anything. Francis stood up, did the drinking gesture with his left hand, pulled on his cigarette with the right. 'Drink?'

Jesús stopped looking around and faced Francis. 'You alright?'

'Yeah, fine.' He gave himself the instructions in his head again. *Stand up straight. Look the guy behind the counter in the eyes. Keep your hands in your pockets so no one can see they're shaking.* Charbel looked at him again. This time for too long. *You are not the boss of me,* Francis thought. *You are not the boss.* 'Beer?'

'Yeah.' Jesús got out his phone. Francis knew he was trying to work out if the women in the bar were a better chance of a hook-up than the girl he'd been texting with. Francis moved towards the bar where a woman with dark roots and bright blond hair was wiping the counter with a rag.

'What can I get you?' she shouted over the music. AC/DC started up with 'Back in Black'. It was definitely retro night.

'Three schooners of New.'

The woman pulled out three frosted glasses and began to fill them up. One of the frizzy-haired women leaned against the bar next to him, sipped her pink Bacardi in its bottle. She didn't look so bad up close. Too much makeup but he wasn't picky. Her clothes said she'd been at work all day. The ID card she used to get into work was still clipped to her pants. She was tapping out the rhythm of the song with her hands on the bar.

He could feel the words vibrating underneath his feet. The woman behind the bar put his drinks in front of him. He brushed up against the woman with the frizzy hair on purpose when he went to pay. She turned and looked at him. They made eye contact. Where to go from here? He was pretty shit at this but it wasn't for lack of trying.

He smiled. She smiled back. He ran his hands down the front of his shirt to smooth out the creases. 'You like AC/DC?'

'Yeah, they're alright.' She nodded, looked him up and down.

'My dad knew AC/DC, like back in the day, before they were all famous and shit.'

She looked at him. Raised her eyebrows. Disbelieving. Never tell a real story that sounds like it isn't true. 'Is that right?'

'Yeah. They were in Villawood together, back before it was Villawood, like now. They came from Scotland and my dad came from Italy. They lived together.'

'Your dad's in Villawood?'

'Not like it is now, like it was before the refugees. With just regular migrants.'

'Regular,' she said. She nodded her head. The music just kept on getting louder. He wasn't sure she'd heard a word. She looked at him like he was a wanker. He was a wanker. Shitty pickup line. He needed to work on something better. He realised just how much he was moving: swaying from side to side. Some guy pushed up against his back to get towards the bar. He looked towards the guy and then the girl was gone. Shit.

He pushed the beers into a triangle. Held them with his hands. Tried to give it all his concentration but couldn't. He was looking for the girl with the frizzy hair. Where did she go? He should have started with, 'What's your name?' 'My dad's a regular guy from Villawood.' Fuck. What kind of pickup line was that? Maybe he could find her. Buy her a drink. She was interested, maybe.

His hands shook again. He turned with the three beers. Pushed them straight into some big bloke's chest and watched as the beer jumped out of his hands and all over his shirt and down the other bloke's pants.

'Shit.'

Two hands jumped out at him from the enormous body, pushed him backwards and then he was on the floor, and a giant foot kicked him in the stomach. He was wet all over. He thought his insides must have burst open and were soaking through his shirt. He ran his hand over his stomach, checked it for blood. It was beer. It was only the beer he spilled.

'Fuckin' cunt,' someone was yelling from above. He was so small down here, everyone else was huge. And then someone got their hands up under his armpits and he was being dragged across the floor.

'Get up. Get up.' He couldn't work out where all the instructions were coming from until someone pulled him onto a chair. It was the bouncer. He remembered his instructions to himself: *Get your ID out, look them in the eyes, be cool.*

This big black face was all up in his and was saying, 'I'm going to have to ask you to leave.' And Francis was looking from his big stern eyes in real time to the ID tag he was wearing around his neck. The face on the tag was smiling. The face in front of him was not.

'Yeah, yeah. Leave.' *Look him in the eye, like you're not high or anything.* Charbel took his left arm. Jesús took his right. He was out in the night air and the bright lights of Church Street again, just like that, before he could even understand how he got there.

'Can I sit down?'

'No.'

Jesús and Charbel were dragging him down the street.

'Walk.'

He started to use his legs. His head was thumping. He walked. They were back in front of the library before he was allowed to sit down on the steps.

Charbel was huffing and puffing in front of him. 'You almost got bashed.'

Francis watched him look around like there might be someone waiting to hit him again.

'Fuck. Why do you always do that?'

'Do what?'

'Make people want to bash you?'

'I never did nothing.' Francis ran his hands over his body just to make sure all his parts were still there. It was true. He never did anything really, but he was always getting into fights. He just had something about him. Something that said *bash me*.

Hours later, when Mrs. Consalvo came home, they were sprawled out on her flowery couch again, ordinary as a *Neighbours* episode. Mrs. Consalvo was too tired to talk in the mornings. Francis watched as she came through the doorway, paused to run her hand across the image of her husband who went missing all those years ago. In the kitchen she turned the radio on to the Spanish news. In the living room she sat and ate toast, leaning against Jesús' shoulder. Francis shoved his shaking hands deep into his pockets. The boys watched TV and laughed and talked about shit.

2.

Antonio still had one leg that moved properly (the right) and an arm that functioned (also the right) so he got in the car and drove after Rose had gone to sleep. Since the accident he had stopped being a morning person and turned into a night one. He slept late into the day. No more waking up at four in the morning to get to work. He wandered the streets on his crutches.

Tonight, he started out where his downfall began, with the building of the first McMansion in Australia, Old Government House in 1799. To the outsider all these things may seem unrelated but in his mind it all made sense. It wasn't far. He drove down Victoria Road and up O'Connell Street and entered Parramatta Park through the main gates next to the RSL. He couldn't smoke and drive at the same time anymore. He didn't have enough good arms. He parked on the roadside and looked up to where Old Government House sat in the darkness up on its hill. Light spilled from the back where the restaurant was still open. An elderly couple walked out of the restaurant holding hands and slowly wandered down the street. Antonio wound down his window, lit his cigarette, exhaled.

He'd gone on a tour of Old Government House when they'd opened it up to the public not so many years after he built his own home in Parramatta. He'd thought the place was going to be a whole lot more than it was, but in the end it was all illusion. Wooden Greek pillars covered in paint and sand to look like sandstone. Wooden floorboards painted in small squares and lacquered to look like tiles. Wooden countertops with contrasting layers of coloured paint so they looked like marble. This was Australia: marble and granite and sandstone that was really just cheap old wood.

All those years later when Fat Frank drove him out to the acres and acres of nothing where he wanted to build houses that had roofs with no eaves and plastic pipes glued together instead of copper pipes, stick-on yellow fake windowpane strips, stick-on shutters, stick-on chimneys and polystyrene frames for the slabs, he thought of Old Government House. He should have known Fat Frank was right when he said those houses would sell. Everyone here wanted to live in joke houses, even the leaders of the country. Fat Frank thought he invented the McMansion but it was really Mrs. Macquarie when she moved into Old Government House and wanted all those things like the sandstone and marble and tiles she couldn't afford, so she faked it.

Antonio flicked his cigarette butt out the window and watched it land on the ground. He unfurled the fingers on the only hand that worked right. He thought about the undertaker preparing Nico's body, the cleaning of his skin, dressing him in his good navy suit. He thought about how histories could be written on bodies. Nico had always had bumps and scars, places where the skin was uneven.

He checked the glove box to make sure he had another pack and he did, squashed under the small bottle of whisky he kept there too, for his night-time driving. Of course, he didn't drink it while he was driving, just when he stopped, when he'd settled in for a few hours in a cul-de-sac or a side street. These were the places he drove to, to think about what he was going to do about everything. Other people, they went to the beach or a river or a mountain full of trees when they just wanted to stare out into space and think. Antonio, he liked looking at houses, streets too, but mostly houses.

He started the ignition, bashed the gear back into drive with his elbow. He drove up onto the highway and cut across to Woodville Road, headed south-west towards another of the places where he'd begun. He drove. During the day Woodville Road was always full, always loud, the houses had people on their verandahs, people parked on the sidewalk in front of the small shops. Children skipped on their way to school. At night, the whole place went quiet. The landscape was so flat you could see right out to the horizon, no place for anything to hide. He took a long hard look at the houses when he was stopped at red lights. Sometimes he stayed there and looked for more than one red light. If there wasn't anyone behind him he'd stay for two or three red lights, just staring until his eyes were full up with the place. There were the Queenslanders stuck too far south, and the places made from shit-brown bricks sitting in their squat squares, and the odd McMansion with its Greek columns and gold-plated exterior fittings sitting like a giant 'fuck you' in between two fibro houses with walls you could break through with a kitchen spoon. Giant rectangles of brick apartment blocks three to four storeys high broke everything up with their straight, straight lines. It pissed him off, the disorder of the place. Sometimes when he looked at things like this it made a lot of sense how everyone around here wanted to move sideways—not out of the community, just to the nearest estate where they could be in the community but not *in the community*, where everything was given a bit of symmetry and all the chaos got locked out at the gate.

Not too far from here, behind Villawood Station, was where he'd first met Nico, but he wouldn't go there now. Instead, he kept driving, drove until he ended up at the same place he ended up most nights. He came around the back way and entered down the side of one of the last houses that was being built. He couldn't go through the front gate. The security guard knew him now, had told him last time that he shouldn't be coming around at night anymore. 'On account of you don't live here,' he'd said. 'And,' he'd added, 'you don't even work here anymore.'

He may not work here anymore but he still knew that this was Lot Number 185 that he had his car parked in front of, and that the security guard wasn't moving from that gatehouse unless the little TV he kept in the corner blew up.

To his left was where the new residents lived, all oversized houses shoved up too close to one another, the lights were still on in some of them. To his right there was nothing and nothing and nothing. Fat Frank was behind schedule. Antonio could see it from here. It would give Nico some satisfaction to know that he had caused all this lateness.

'Sixty days, sixty days.' It was Fat Frank's mantra as the site manager, none of the McShitboxes should take more than sixty days before the basics of walls and flooring were up.

Antonio fished the whisky out of his glove box, shoved the bottle between his thighs and unscrewed the lid with his good hand. He got out of the car, leaned up against it, looked up at the sky and back to Lot 185 and took a deep drink. The house was still half finished, still had the yellow tape that the guys from WorkCover had used to cordon off the investigation site around the scaffolding lying on its front lawn.

Lot 185 was *The Aspire*. Its selling point was its fifty per cent glass frontage. 'Rooms Filled With Natural Light!' the brochure said. Fat Frank had come up with that himself. That's why he was the site manager and Antonio wasn't anymore, because he could cut the costs of building a place in half by replacing bricks with much cheaper materials like glass and then he could work out how to sell it to the customer like it was something they wanted: 'Rooms Filled With Natural Light!'

That kind of shit was always bringing Antonio down but it was Lot 185 that finally undid him after forty years in the construction industry. If he was being honest with himself maybe he'd admit that it was really something that started a long time before, maybe even as far back as those early days on the factory floor with Nico, maybe even further back than that.

It might have started back in the Nissen huts at the Villawood Migrant Hostel. Nico had it down, even then—the ability to stand larger than other people. Nico had arrived in Australia not too long before Antonio, but he knew about things like where to look for a job and what land to build on and how you talk to Australians.

The weight of the heat inside the huts had drawn everyone to the yard, even in winter when it was damp and mouldy and the whole place smelled like shit. There were English and Irish and Italian and Polish and German and Greek, entire villages from places he'd never been to just *materialised* like that, out of nowhere. Nico walked the perimeter and Antonio walked with him. Nico knew exactly when Antonio's mind wandered off to some dark place. When that happened, Nico touched him silently on the upper arm. They walked. Nico brought him back.

Everyone knew who Nico was, of course. But on the day Nico died he was fat and graceless and no one wanted to listen to what he had to say. They laughed at him when he walked across the construction site. Nico had become a nobody and part of that nobodiness had rubbed off on Antonio.

If he could he'd ask Nico to forgive him but it was probably far too late for that. Antonio took another of the painkillers his doctor gave him out of his pocket and swallowed it with a gulp of his whisky. He kicked a loose piece of concrete on the ground with one of his crutches. He had that tightrope sensation again, that terrible hunger for air. He crouched down slowly and picked up the loose pieces of cement lying there. One by one, he threw them at the newly fitted windows and watched the glass crack in spirals.

Nico showed up beside him. He looked light, unbroken. He had a bucket of concrete chips and they threw them together at that house, at the eaves on the roof, at the gold plate they had started applying on the stair railings. Nico shook his head. He'd survived the Allied forces bombing his village three times, had taken a boat to the other side of the world, worked twelve hours a day, made something of himself. And now he'd come undone.

He said, 'You know, I was everything they told me to be, I did the jobs they told me to do, never complained, worked hard, stopped speaking my own language, looked the other way when they called me names. Now, everything is different, what a waste. They laugh at me when I speak.'

In some part of his mind, Antonio had known what would happen if he tried to lift Nico that day after his fall on Lot 185, but it was too late to stop all that from happening now, and it was only just the beginning.

3

7:30 A.M. Friday. Clare walked because she liked to walk. It didn't matter that it took her an hour from Surry Hills to Newtown. She liked looking. The women in tight skirts went barefoot on Devonshire and Belvoir, carrying their heels home from the nightclubs on Oxford Street. She walked under the overhangs of shops and looked through their windows at full-skirted 60s dresses, bright red plastic underwear, posters about the hazards of cigarette butts finding their way into drain pipes, people who spent hours in coffee shops reading newspapers and books. She was born to these city streets, even though she wasn't really born in the city; she was made to be born here and when she walked these streets she told herself that she was.

Someone who *was* really born in the city—her mother. Clare knew exactly which terrace she had lived in but she could never picture her there. When her mother described the home she grew up in, it was always a dull and grey and silent image in which she was in a threadbare pinafore next to her stony, ruddy-faced English mother, no smiles to be seen.

Now, someone had picked out the details of the window frames and guttering in a bright blue. On the bottom balcony there were long rectangular pots of herbs and on the top-floor balcony they had a wrought-iron set of two red chairs and a table with a giant Buddha face hanging from the wall behind. Walking past there at night, Clare could often see the shadows of people behind the windows. Behind the front-door grates they had bicycles with baskets on the front like the ones women in French movies ride to the markets. Her father still called her mother 'Rose of the Hills' when he was feeling affectionate, as though she was from some far-flung mountain village and not here, not impossibly hip Surry Hills.

Clare stepped onto Cleveland Street; a dog barked somewhere. She was going to be relaxed today. She had resolved not to get uptight about anything. Last night she had called home several times to speak to her little brother. At twenty-three Francis was not really little anymore, but Clare could not seem to think of him as anything but a perpetual adolescent. Perhaps it was the seven-year gap between them, or perhaps it was because he was so damn immature—either way, in her mind, he was always in primary school, always in school shorts with his socks pulled up to his knees. Her father's retirement party—why should she even need to remind him that it was this Saturday? In the house in which Francis still lived? She turned onto City Road. Not her problem. She was not going to worry about anything today.

In Parramatta, right now, her father would be sitting on a chair on his concrete front lawn, arms folded across his chest. Her mother would be sitting on a chair on the front lawn of their neighbour Lucy's perpetually half-built house, drinking tea and eating macaroons and joining in a running commentary on everyone that walked down the street. Her brother would still be out of it, getting over the night before.

Here, walking down King Street, things were quiet. The only people out were small men with big dogs and women with dreadlocks and yoga mats. King Street! You could lose yourself here somewhere between a second-hand clothes shop and a Thai restaurant. She liked to read all the posters on the light poles as she walked by them. There were share houses that needed a sixth roommate and Socialist Alliance meetings about freeing the refugees and bands full of boys with long faces and pouty lips. 'Interesting,' her mother always said in response to everything she saw here. It was her mother's favourite word, *interesting*.

At the bookshop she unlocked the door, turned the sign around to 'Yes, We're Open' and switched on the lights. The first few customers drifted into the shop around nine. Always, it was middle-aged women at this time of day. They came in and ran their fingers up and down the spines of books and carefully considered their covers. She knew this kind of woman. They were looking for the book that would define who they were, the book of their life. It wasn't there. She could save them the time and money by telling every one of these forty-something women outright, but they'd never believe her. She took their money and wrapped their books in brown paper bags. They believed in stories.

At ten, things went down a different road entirely. He walked in, a Vietnamese kid looking no older than fifteen, with his tight jeans and Vans sneakers. He walked straight up to the counter and looked startled once he arrived, like he'd taken a wrong turn and gotten lost.

'Oh Miss,' he said, trying to shove his fists into the too-tight spaces of his jean pockets. 'Miss Martone.' He smiled and stood there looking at her. Clare smiled back. She could never remember their names, not even when she was still teaching. She tried but there wasn't enough space in her head after she'd learnt everything there was about every book, made matching worksheets and scrawled red marks across her students' essays. As if it mattered; it didn't matter in the end, what she really needed was the ability to put names to faces.

'Hi,' Clare fingered her name tag feeling embarrassed, like she'd been exposed.

'You don't remember me, do you?' He had the kind of hair that was becoming trendy among the metrosexuals on King Street—that long sweep of fringe to one side that constantly needed to be flipped out of the eyes. He was thin, impossibly tall. His pants sank too low below his abdomen.

'I was in your class, Year Ten, about six years ago.'

'Right.' That year, her first year of teaching, was a bit of a blur. 'I do remember you but I'm not sure I remember your name.' It was the line she used when she was caught on the outside.

'Paul. Paul Nguyen.'

'Right, well nice to see you again Paul, best of luck with everything.' She smiled a short sweet smile and then looked in the other direction. This was the part where they were meant to go away so she could stop feeling like she was on display.

He put on a face like he'd been caught doing the wrong thing before he stammered. 'I'm here to work. I start today. Ben hired me.'

'Right,' she said. But it was not right. Ben should have known better.

She didn't want her past around her today, so she sent him off—to the storeroom to unpack and tick off books, to the back shelves that needed sorting and cleaning, to the coffee shop around the corner. But every time she sent him off he was back again asking what he could do next. One time when he came back to the counter she thought she could remember him for a second, some image of him being quiet and alone on the playground with a book. Quiet and alone: he had the words stamped all over him. Vietnamese, but he didn't hang with the maths kids. He was usually alone.

He called her Miss throughout the day, even though she asked him not to, and he spoke quietly, like he was in a library. She watched him, absorbed in a graphic novel, turning the pages carefully, until he remembered not being alone, and put it back on the shelf. When she looked at his face she could see that he looked older than she had originally thought. There was a faint line beginning in the middle of his forehead.

The rest of the day was much the same. In between customers

she flipped through the pages of a coffee-table book on houses and considered buying it as a retirement gift for her father. He liked houses, building them, looking at them. She would like to know what had happened at the site of the last one he was building. Then again, maybe she didn't want to know the whole story, not exactly. It didn't make sense when he was trying to explain it to her from his hospital bed, something about the importance of dignity. Then again, her father had never made much sense to her.

Their shifts ended at the same time. She stayed back, closed down the cash register and locked the back doors. When she walked out of the shop he was still there staring at the display in the window.

'Well,' she said, looking at him, standing there, inspecting the books on display in the window as if he'd never seen a bookshop before. 'That's it for the day.' She wasn't so sure what else she needed to say to him. He hung around and looked from the books in the window and back to her again.

When she began to walk, he walked beside her. He didn't say anything, just walked, his feet dragging, too heavy, his Vans going slip slap on the pavement. She wondered if he was waiting for instructions. She felt the need to say something, 'How are you getting home?'

'Train, another train, walk.'

'You still live near Parramatta then?'

'Yeah. Near there, Merrylands.'

'Long way for a part-time job.'

Slip, slap. They walked down King Street towards the train station. 'You don't teach anymore then?'

'No. I work in a *bookshop*.' The condescending tone of her voice made her wince at her words. These were the things that he wasn't understanding: that she was not a patient person, that she was a very efficient teacher but not a loving one, that she had left that all behind when she moved to the city. This was her life now. Alright? She didn't need to explain it to anyone.

Even Paul's feet next to her had gone quiet. She had this effect on people sometimes. She tried to be nicer.

'So why are you working all the way in the city then?' she asked.

'My parents think I'm studying law at Sydney Uni but I dropped out—I thought, well, at least I could get a job in the city, you know. It feels a little less like I'm lying when I leave the house every day.'

He pulled on the black spikes of his hair. 'I like books.'

'My parents think I'm still a teacher,' she said softly and made a point of looking him in the eyes like she was really listening.

So here they were, former teacher, former student, both liars.

'Well, here we are,' he said and smiled. 'I'll see you at work next week.'

She shouldn't have told him anything that personal. She felt embarrassed by it now and even though he wasn't in front of her, she knew her face was turning red. She watched him go as he turned and headed towards the stairs at Newtown Station.

4.

Now that Antonio wasn't getting up early, neither was Rose. She wasn't sleeping that well anyway. When her husband left their home late at night, a sense of absence woke her. He thinks she doesn't know what he gets up to. She even followed him the other night, watched him throwing things into the windows of half-built houses. Once, she had had to collect Francis from a police station when he was caught doing the same thing. Antonio was disappointed that Francis didn't grow into the same man he was, but he didn't realise they were two sides of the same coin. She knew a lot of things her husband did not. This is the problem with men, her friend Lucy always said; they think women know nothing.

Other things he thought she didn't know—that those letters just kept on arriving, the ones from WorkCover, from the bank, from the construction company, from the CFMEU, from the police, from some legal company that sent out envelopes printed with crushed cars and the slogan 'No Win, No Fee'. He shoved them under the bed as if all this business would go away if no one read them. But Rose did.

From those letters she now knew they had three investment properties, not just the one she didn't want in the first place: 12 Woodlands Drive, Villawood; 8 Blackheath Drive, Smithfield; and 67 West Fairfield Road, Fairfield. She predicted that the two new additions would be like the first—old sturdy brick of the 1960s era, a quarter-acre block. Antonio was more sure of these kinds of houses than he'd ever been

NO MORE BOATS · 43

sure of anything, but when the first one was set on fire they'd almost gone broke. She got it. They'd both come from nothing and he wanted something better than that. But at what cost? Mortgaging, remortgaging. He took imaginary money and put it into bricks and mortar, which must have looked close enough to his idea of real wealth.

It didn't seem to make their real lives any better. Not that she'd had much to complain about until now.

While the morning crept into the early afternoon, Rose watched him sleeping. People didn't talk about men having beauty, but her husband was a beautiful man, even at this age, more beautiful than she ever was. His body still had a lean, olive-coloured symmetry. In her mind, she'd had him hundreds of times, in the park, in the car, at work, before she'd ever had him in the flesh. She had met him at sixteen. She recalled being full of desire and invincible back then; remembered feeling exactly this: that if she married this man, she would always be this way.

She got out of bed, wrapped her nightgown tightly over her body and made her way downstairs. Her family had left evidence of their presence around the place: the half-moon imprint of Antonio's thumb in the paint in the hallway, the floral blinds Clare helped her to sew, Francis' shoes stranded in the middle of the hallway for the last twenty-three years.

But for now, she felt alone.

In the kitchen downstairs the dishes from last night's meal were still in the sink. She stared at their soggy innards before plunging her hands into the now cold water and pulling the plug. Don't think she hadn't noticed his eyes looking at those dishes when she had just left them last night. If he could have put his plastered arm into the sink and done them himself he would have. The problem with Antonio was he'd mistaken her for some sort of domestic woman from the very beginning. Not such a hard thing for him to imagine—he had watched her for two years working in the industrial kitchen of the Villawood Migrant Hostel before he got up the nerve to ask her out.

But Antonio hadn't looked at what she was doing closely enough. Rose was never afraid to lift heavy pots, chop pounds and pounds of vegetables, to stand in the summer's heat under corrugated iron, in front of a stove. What she never liked was the cleaning, the feel of her arms reaching down into sinks full of murky water littered with the remnants of food, or kneeling on cold, tiled floors, scrubbing; the smell of harsh chemicals and the carbolic and bleach forever stuck to her skin.

When she'd been over the sink, up to her elbows in suds, she had often thought of her mother. Her mother had believed in very little other than that the Japanese were going to invade during the war, and that one's home should always be clean and sanitary. Her mother hadn't loved people so much as she kept them clean, which to her had probably been a kind of love in itself. Perhaps that's why Rose's father had left them. She didn't blame him and her mother didn't seem to care any-way—she just opened up her doors and turned the terrace they were renting into a boarding house for all those men, shattered and needing a cheap bed after the war. Together, they'd cleaned up after them. If she could go back in time she'd ask both her parents if it was worth it, upending their lives from one slum town in England for another slum town in Australia, but her mother was gone and she'd never found out what happened to her father.

So, because Rose loved Antonio, she cleaned for him.

In a few hours she'd have this place clean, full of food and full of guests. She knew Antonio didn't want the retirement party, that he had in fact been forced into retirement, though he had never actually admitted that in front of her. But she also knew the party was a good thing. It always made him a stronger man, being the centre of attention.

She polished the wood on the kitchen table and laid out

bowls of olives and nuts and glasses for the wine and beer. She was cutting cucumber sandwiches into small slivers when Francis entered the kitchen in his boxer shorts, his naked chest so broad at the top that he blocked the kitchen doorway. She watched him looking at the plastic-wrapped dishes of food laid out on the kitchen counter, surveying the card tables folded and leaning up against the kitchen wall, ready to be laid out in the lounge room; she watched as he put these things together in his mind and remembered what was happening today.

'Welcome!' she said, turning to him with a knife in one hand, a mitt in the other, her blond hair wrapped up in a scarf to keep it from getting dirty. Sometimes when she looked at her children like this, she got a glimpse of what she must look like to them. To Francis she must look like a housewife in a 1950s movie.

'Ohhh . . . too loud this early in the morning.'

'It's twelve.'

Francis turned and removed the milk from the fridge and the Weet-Bix and sugar from the cupboard before sitting down on the bench stool in front of her, where he ate and grunted and watched her work.

'I'll need your help today. I need you to take around plates and fill up people's glasses.'

'Yep. Done.'

Antonio had slipped into the back garden. She could see him from the kitchen window pruning tomato vines with his one good hand. It had always been the place where he was most calm, pruning, picking. She never talked to him when he was in that space. She imagined, in his head, he was probably somewhere in the past. When she turned back to Francis he was gone, as always. The only evidence of his having been there was a half-eaten bowl of Weet-Bix.

At four the bell rang. Rose went to the door to answer it. Clare stood there looking fresh and confident in a red dress and brown suede shoes. She cut her hair in a bob these days, just like Rose did, with blond highlights in front. At these times Rose was so glad that Clare had gotten over trying to prove some point at university by having dirty dreadlocked hair and baggy shirts with no bra.

'Hi,' she said walking into the room and hanging her cardigan over a chair. 'What can I help you with?' This was Clare, always ready to go, mind on the task ahead.

'Well there's the quiches on the counter in the kitchen, they need to be put in the oven and there's some more beer in the garage that needs to be brought in.'

'Where's Francis?'

'I've no idea.'

'Honestly,' Clare said, and Rose wondered if she'd ever get a child of her own to fuss over the way she fussed over Francis. Under her arm Clare carried a large rectangular object wrapped in gold paper. Another book, Rose supposed. Clare was always bringing books that no one ever read into the house. Clare left the package on the bench, rolled her sleeves up and headed straight out to the garage.

It had been Rose's idea to have the retirement party. She wanted Antonio to be surrounded with men who spoke loudly and freely, filling the air with themselves. She wanted to bring Antonio out of himself again, to watch him become animated, to watch him talking football and construction and the future.

When she was shopping for the party she had run into Nico's widow, Mona. She used to have a huge, curly head of hair. Now that she'd cut it short there was a fierceness in her face that hadn't been there before. Mona didn't look at her anymore. Not directly, not since the funeral. Rose had tried calling her several times, had left messages that weren't returned. The wife of another builder had called her back eventually and told Rose that Mona couldn't handle talking to her, couldn't handle anyone else's guilt about what had happened, didn't want to feel like she had to make anyone else feel alright again.

It wasn't alright, Mona wanted that specific message to be passed on, *it wasn't alright and there was nothing that Rose or the CFMEU or the guys from workers' comp or any of those people who came around with flowers or endless trays of food could do about it.* Rose and Mona had raised their children together, at all those union family days and barbeques. They'd cried together when their eldest daughters had moved out of home and made jokes about Nico growing fat in his old age and now she'd lost both of them.

Rose had looked through the window at the local hairdressers and seen Mona there. Rose had watched her staring blankly at the mirror in front of her while the woman cut her hair. Mona's disappointment and rage seemed to seep out from her skin so that even a few feet away Rose could feel it. Rose wanted to go up and touch her, to say, *I'm sorry, I'm sorry all the time.*

But she didn't.

5

I t had rained buckets the week before Nico died. It rained so much that work on the estate had slowed down. 'Sixty days, sixty days,' Fat Frank kept saying, but the last one they finished took sixty-eight and the one before that sixty-five. They were running out of indoor jobs when the rain finally let up for a couple of days and they could work outside again.

Everything had a sharp, metallic, earthy smell. Antonio parked behind Lot 185 and walked down the side driveway to where he could see Nico leaning against the chain link fence smoking. Nico was wearing blue pants and an orange hard hat and he didn't try to hide that he was sizing up every man that walked past him. Nico was as he would have been back in 1970 or 1962 or 1958. It was everyone else that was different. Vietnamese. Chinese. Cambodian. Korean. Lebanese, Assyrian, from God knows where. They wore the same uniform of white singlets and cargo pants and black steel-capped boots.

Nico offered Antonio a cigarette at the gate. When Nico raised his hand to light it Antonio could see his roof tiler's hands, the line of calluses across the middle of the palm. Instinctively Antonio looked away and up at the roof. They already had several stacks of tiles up there in neat bundles ready for laying. He watched as the thin figure of a black-haired man climbed quickly up the stairs of the scaffold with half a dozen tiles on his shoulder. More stacks of tiles were deposited on the roof beams. He was back on the roof again with another stack before Antonio could finish his cigarette.

'I'll have the scaffolding up on the other side of the building by about lunchtime today so your guys can tile the other side.' Nico nodded his head and stubbed out his cigarette under the heavy thud of his boot. He was beginning to sweat around the edges of his hat even at this time of the morning. 'See you at lunch.'

Antonio walked off to the other side of the building where the scaffolding parts had been delivered. He counted and checked them off. On the front right-hand corner the stack of tubing had sunk partly into the mud. He would need to lift each piece out later, clean it, stack it back neatly in another place.

Then two of *them* showed up beside him. He'd asked the foreman for someone who was licensed but these two looked fresh off the boat. The foreman had probably subcontracted out to Koreans who had subcontracted out to these Vietnamese or Chinese or whatever they were, poor shits making $400 a week. He had to admit they were fast and strong but they couldn't do things properly. They weren't even trained right. They came from countries where you just whacked up a scaffold with bamboo and string and when everything collapsed you covered up the whole mess by throwing the buildings and bodies into giant holes in the ground and starting again.

Antonio pulled one of the baseplates from the stack and pushed it firmly into the ground with his foot. He grabbed a scaffolding tube and held it vertical above the plate. These things felt heavier all the time. The older-looking one followed him, grabbing a section of tube and bringing it over. He picked it up with his thin arm like it was nothing and said something to the younger one in their language. They were both pulling the tubes and the joiners off the pile, carrying them two and three pieces at a time. The older one inserted his tube into the one Antonio was holding down. When Antonio got close he saw that he knew his face. They'd laid concrete together when they were building the foundations. The other man had looked younger at first, but when you got a good look at him his hair was flecked with grey. The skin of his face was papery and dry. Building sites were full of these kinds of faces without names.

They could follow what he was doing, mostly. Maybe they were strong, he'd give them that, but he didn't like how they did things. Twice he stopped them and pulled apart what they did, told them to do it again. He put the spirit level on top of one of the bars and pulled the younger one over to show him how it was slightly off a perfect horizontal. The guy looked at the tacky fake Rolex that OH&S forbade him from wearing on the building site.

'I don't give a shit if it takes you longer,' Antonio said, but the guy didn't understand or pretended not to. Either way, he got on with it. They did the job, he checked the job, sometimes he tore their job apart.

12:00. It was lunchtime and he was starving. Antonio got his lunch from the trailer and found Nico above him on a scaffold supervising the tiling. From down here he could see the fold of Nico's belly protruding over his pants as he walked back and forth across the scaffold.

Nico and Antonio sat on a bench in front of the apartment block. Sometimes by lunchtime they were too tired to talk much, but they didn't really want to admit it. It didn't matter so much anymore though. They were the last of their kind. There was no one else to talk to, really; they had outlasted all the other people like them. Now the young Aussies sat with the children of people like them who had migrated too long ago for anyone to remember that they were migrants too. If he ever saw Francis out there on the site, he was sitting with this group. Antonio could never work out where he was during the day; he always stayed away from him at work. The Vietnamese sat together. The Chinese. The everything-elses: they all sat together. The three Arab Muslim guys kept to themselves.

'That's not right,' Nico said, looking up at the roof above where the two men continued to finish the scaffold. They were at the top now but they shouldn't have been, Antonio thought. They hadn't put the vertical safety bracing on each level of the scaffold before they climbed to the next one. It wasn't safe. The whole thing could fall apart. He was about to say something, but the scaffold wasn't what Nico was looking at.

'The roof beams. They don't look level. Can't get tiles on uneven roof beams.'

Antonio needed to go to the toilet. 'Yeah,' he said, but he wasn't sure about the beams from here. It was too hard to tell. Sometimes things just looked a little sideways when you were staring at them from below. Nico was more of a roof man than him.

'I'll be back.'

In the portaloo there were competing half-naked women of varying shapes and colours. He liked the big-breasted woman with the dark hair and something that looked like Russian scrawled at the bottom of the poster. A Korean girl in a tartan skirt and pigtails checked him out while he peed.

When Antonio returned to the bench Nico was gone but his food was still there. Antonio didn't see where he was until he heard the sound of metal buckling. He looked up to see Nico on top of the scaffolding on the fourth platform up. Nico should have known better than to get up on a scaffold that didn't have all its footings attached yet. It wasn't stable. Antonio could see even from here that Nico's heavy body was throwing everything out of alignment. The entire scaffold was slowly bending back away from the building.

Nico looked frozen there on the top platform. Someone

shouted something. The emergency bell rang. Nico slid too quietly off the fourth platform as the entire scaffold continued to bend forward towards the ground and then began to break apart. The wooden beams of each platform fell separately and hit each other in midair as the metal tubing they were sitting on bent to the point where there was nothing securing them anymore.

Antonio didn't remember Nico's body in the air, couldn't recall how it got from fifteen metres up all the way down to the ground. But he did remember Nico lying there on the concrete, his hat torn off by the fall, his comb-over all out of place and the large crack of his arse falling out of his pants. The foreman came running through the yard, yelling 'get back' and pushing groups of men away from where the scaffold was collapsing. Some ran. Some stared; if Nico was conscious he would have screamed at them, told them all to stop looking.

Later, Antonio might've realised that it wasn't the most important thing to do, maybe not even to Nico. But right then his duty was clear, specific; it presented itself. He walked right up underneath the leaning scaffold where Nico's body lay. He was going to lift Nico, gently, his whole body, turn him around and push his hair and his pants back into place. He didn't want anyone smiling at Nico, didn't want anyone laughing; he thought he owed him this. He crouched over his friend's back. It was a short lift. He squatted. He worked his arms under Nico's torso, surprised by the coolness of his body. For half a second his faith was unwavering and he turned with Nico's body in his arms; they were almost there, and then something shifted above him—Nico's belly pushed against his chest, and something else followed, a piece of metal tubing from the sky; Nico's right arm slipped from his grasp—and he knew, close as they were, they'd never make it; an inch, a centimetre, a whole lifetime lost. And still Antonio held him, but there was no way, he felt his leg twist back. All one hundred and fifty kilos of Nicolai Molazzo pinned him to the concrete.

The sky exploded. Metal rained down. Antonio felt the bones in his arm shoot from the inside to the outside of his flesh. He began to scream, his face shoved into Nico's belly. Nico who in the last few years had insisted that he had done enough listening, he would not listen to anyone again, not ever.

In the hospital Antonio drifted in and out of consciousness. The nurse showed him how to operate the button on the IV when the pain came back.

'You know what I did?' he said when Francis was standing over him.

'Everyone knows what you did, Dad.'

He slept. He woke up. Rose brought in wet cloths to wipe his face. The man from WorkCover wanted him to explain it again, how it happened. He wanted to know if it was worth it: the risk, the loss, the exchange. An arm and a leg for Nico's dignity. The *idea* of his dignity.

6.

Yes. Francis had arrived late. Fairly predictable. But he was here now, so everyone could just chill. Alright? He and Jesús had entered from the backyard so that Francis could pretend he'd been there for ages without being seen. *I've just been outside checking on the tomatoes, right? Sorry I didn't see ya, Mum. Been here for ages. Ages.*

Jesús was wearing a bad paisley tie that was knotted too tightly. Francis should have worn a tie too. These were the things that Jesús always had down and Francis didn't. Jesús was all into showing respect for your parents and their friends, at least in front of them.

'Look at those fat fucks of watermelons,' Jesús said as they passed through the garden. He stopped and kicked one lightly. There was the hollow sound of it against his toe.

His dad's friends had been sent to the back verandah to smoke. John Farnham kept screaming out the sliding glass doors every time they were opened. They stood there with their potato faces sucking on cigarettes.

'Aye, Francis!' One of the men said as he got closer. He grabbed Francis on the shoulders, leaned in and kissed him on both cheeks. These men always kissed. 'You've grown.' They always said that too.

He grabbed each man's fist. Wrapped his two hands around their one hand and shook hard like he meant it, like his dad taught him to.

'This is my friend Jesús.' The circle of men smiled and nodded their heads and shook Jesús' hand too hard.

'How's it going?' Peter said to Francis, whacking him hard on his right arm. 'You taking care of your dad?'

He worked with Peter on site. He was one of the older guys, one of the very few of them still around. Greek or something. Too fussy. Too particular. They slowed construction down and talked too much. Their wives sent everyone Christmas cards at the end of the year like it was 1952 or something. He looked at the sunspots on Peter's hands as he leaned, tired, against the back wall and smoked, nodding at everyone who entered and exited through the back like he was some sort of pretty con-man. Francis would be glad when they all retired. It didn't matter how the guys like Peter treated him, they still made him feel like he was a kid because they'd known him when he was one. Francis lit up because it was easier than talking. He leaned up against the cement wall and the wood pylons and got on with the business of smoking.

Inside the party, things were rolling. His mum was sitting with the wives' club on the couches in the corner of the living room. They were sitting with their legs crossed and their various shades of pink lipstick, drinking sherry. Great-uncle Mark, with his slow feet and the IQ of a four-year-old, danced with Clare. His father positioned himself on the outside but somehow also at the centre of the group of men. He was telling stories. Francis could tell even from this side of the room that he was doing that thing where he picked out each person individually and told their stories to the rest. The men smiled and nodded as they heard Antonio recount each anecdote, each one bigger and more impressive than the last.

In the kitchen Francis and Jesús took beers out of the melting ice in the sink. John Farnham asked questions from the stereo speakers:

What about the world around us?

How can we fail to see?
What about the age of reason?

'Francis. Jesús. You're here.' His mother had appeared from nowhere.

'Been here ages, Mum. Just talking to everyone.'

She ignored her son completely, turned to Jesús and gave him a kiss. 'I hear you are doing very, very well for yourself. Worked hard. Almost an accountant now. An accountant. Your mother will be able to visit you in your office one day.'

Jesús smiled and nodded. But Francis knew his mother was not really speaking to Jesús. She was speaking to him. She wanted him to be more like Jesús. To have dreams of offices too. Never going to happen. Francis smiled at her. He knew his mother well enough. He knew that she'd had just the right amount of sherry and was enjoying herself just enough to smile back at him eventually, if he kept on smiling.

She turned her back on him, began pulling plates out of the fridge, removed plastic wrapping, and revealed tiny sandwiches and small swirls of purple and green. She did all this without looking at Francis. He was late to his father's party and he did not want to work in an office and therefore he would be punished.

'Right.' She put a plate of food in Jesús' hands almost before he could get his arms out to support it. She poked the rim of another plate into Francis' chest. 'Go and serve your father and his friends.'

'Yep.' Francis stood there and smiled and waited until his mother cracked it. She treated him like a guest who had overstayed his welcome. She smiled a kind of lopsided smile he knew was an attempt to stay looking angry at him, 'Go.'

And so Francis and Jesús did what they'd done at their parents' parties since they could walk. They were the servants. They served. They were polite and sometimes even charming. They sneaked shots of the cognac his father's friends brought, and they got drunk without anyone even noticing. They knew all the moves. A man who might have been Greek, or possibly Italian or French (who knew? Francis could never tell the difference) grabbed his mother by the hand and insisted that they dance as Farnham worked his way up to the crescendo of 'The Voice.'

His mother's friend Lucy put her arm around his shoulder and said, 'The man of the house.' Her slight Polish accent sometimes turned her 'th' sounds into 'd' sounds after too much drink so that she sounded like some aging white gangster when she said it, *da man of de house.*

This was Lucy at her best, more like the older sister you wished you had than your mum's best friend.

'Now you should go and introduce yourself to Mrs. Muscas over there. She has a beautiful daughter. Not too much younger than yourself.' Lucy raised her eyebrows at him like she was letting him in on some great secret. She still had the kind of bright blue eyes and fine skin most people would consider beautiful. Even at her age. There was something that Francis had always found so attractive about her but it wasn't necessarily about her looks. It was more about the way she talked to his father, like underneath whatever words came out of her mouth she was really always saying, *I won't take shit from you so don't even try it.* His father had always hated her. Francis could never understand where that conflict had begun.

He shrugged his shoulders and said, 'Maybe I should ask her for a photo then.' He was sure the daughter would be fat.

He worked his way across the living room with the plate and the serviettes and the toothpicks his mother had given him so that people could spear the little swirly things he was carrying. The house was getting louder. Lucy had changed the CD to Julio Iglesias. More people dancing now.

Bob from across the road yelled, 'Aye, Francis bring that

over here.' He was a big man. He nodded his meaty head and listened to what the other four men were saying.

Francis broke into their circle with his plate of food. They were talking Tampa. Suddenly everyone is an expert on boat people. Everyone. Pass the plate. Of course we came by boats too. Can I have one of those toothpicks? But it was a different kind of boat. A serviette? On account of what they did to John Newman we shouldn't let any more in. But they're not Asian anymore. They're Arabs. Can you go get me a beer, son? They're Muslim this time. Like the ones on the news who raped the white girl, just like them.

Jesús walked up to the circle from the other side. 'Last one,' he said holding up a plate with a single sausage roll on it. Bob grabbed for it and stuck it in his mouth in one bite.

Then Francis and Jesús were in the kitchen and no one at the party was paying attention to them anymore and someone had left a half-open bottle of bourbon next to the sink. Francis poured them each half a plastic cup.

They knocked their plastic cups against each other and drank it straight. Jesús put his cup out and waited for Francis to pour another. Francis watched as his hand swayed. This time they sipped their drinks. Takin' it easy. They pulled themselves up onto the kitchen bench and sat on top of it the same way his mum had been telling them not to since they were little kids.

Somehow the party had really got going. Francis could feel the vibrations of the music on the benchtop under their arses. Now Olivia Newton-John and John Farnham were singing together. His mother had the worst taste in music. The worst. His father could never tell the difference between one singer and another. In the next room someone was yelling above the music, 'Dance! Come on, dance!'

Francis realised suddenly there was someone moving around in the walk-in pantry. He looked through the space in between the wooden slats and saw his father stranded there between the boxes of cereal and the canned vegetables. He was looking at a crumpled piece of paper and muttering something silently to himself.

'What are you doing, Dad?' He watched his father look up and smash his head against the naked light bulb in the pantry.

He opened the door. His father stared at him like a kid who had been caught doing something wrong. He fixed the collar of his shirt and said, 'How are you enjoying the party?'

'It's pumpin', Dad. What are you doing in the pantry?'

'I was just trying to get away from everyone, so I could, you know, practise my speech.'

His father prided himself on these kinds of speeches. He was always the one in the family who gave the speeches. Weddings. Christenings. Birthdays. It was strange how these moments made him appear both more vulnerable and stronger at the same time. When he would eventually get up to speak you could see how he fed off the attention of everyone listening to him, how it made him stand in a way that said, I am here and I am significant. But before he got up to speak his father turned into some kind of nervous child who was scared of presenting to his class.

Francis swallowed hard and looked at his father slightly hunched over in the closet so his head wouldn't hit the light bulb above. 'You want to practise on me?'

'No, no. Just, it's alright. I'm almost done. Just wanted to look over my notes and all.' Francis relaxed. He didn't really want to share this kind of intimate moment with his father anyway.

'Right then. We'll leave you to it.' Francis had never been close enough to his father for these kinds of moments not to be awkward. 'Do you want me to tell Mum to turn the music down and get ready for your speech?'

'Yes. Yes. I think that would be good.' His father walked

out to the kitchen and filled up a glass of water in the sink. Francis watched as Jesús jumped off the countertop.

'Mr. Martone.'

'Jesús. Thanks for helping this evening.'

'You're welcome.' Jesús shook his father's hand and smiled like the good ethnic son Francis knew his father had always wanted.

Someone started screaming 'Dance! Dance!' as Francis and Jesús walked back out into the living room. His sister Clare was standing against the back wall telling one of his mum's friends about the kids she was teaching this year. His father's friends had drunk-red faces. His mother sat on a chair in the corner beside Lucy. They crossed their legs tighter, looked at the men and laughed.

Francis pulled aside the empty bottles of beer sitting in front of the stereo and switched off whatever crap was playing. There was a bit of a lull in the noise but mostly people just kept talking. Great-uncle Mark was dancing alone after everyone had left the dance floor.

His father emerged from the kitchen and appeared in the corner of the living room. No notes in his hand. More people stopped talking. Francis got up on a chair at the front of the room and clicked two empty beer bottles together.

'The man himself would like to make a speech. Excuse me, everybody.'

He watched his father approach the front of the room. He nodded at everyone as he walked past them, like he was a king or something. People were too drunk to shut up quickly. Everyone started nudging each other and quiet fell from the front to the back of the room.

'Yeah,' one of his father's workmates was saying to another in the back corner, 'the man was too fat and too old to be climbing up scaffolds, couldn't compete.' The words could just be heard above everything else. Everyone had gone quiet.

It was said just at the point when his father reached the front of the room. Francis watched as he turned slowly and faced everyone.

His face was turning red from the neck upwards. He just stood there breathing. Francis couldn't help but feel nervous at these times. Whatever bad was between them, Francis knew he would always feel this way, tied up in all the anxieties of the man who had raised him. Mostly because he felt like he was the only one who could see them. Even if he chose to ignore them, even if he couldn't talk about them out loud.

His father got the notes he had out of his pocket. He put them back in. 'Fuck you,' he said at last to the entire crowd of people staring at him and walked straight out of the room and back to the kitchen.

No one spoke. His mother left after his father. Clare switched the stereo back on to cover the silence.

No one in his family ever thought that Francis knew anything. He knew they thought he was dumber than a piece of shit and too stoned and that he didn't pay attention. But he knew stuff. He saw the deeper meanings of things. He knew, for example, that his father only got angry when he was ashamed. He knew that his father had always been too ashamed for any ordinary kind of anger.

7.

Going back to the city. Clare was relieved by the prospect of a journey that would probably take her close to an hour and a half in the middle of the day on a Sunday. She'd gone to the party. She'd fulfilled her duty. She'd stayed up until the late hours with her mother cleaning up after Francis had gone out with Jesús and her dad had disappeared. Her mother didn't say anything about what had occurred. Her mother was like that. Pretend it didn't happen and it would go away.

It's not that she didn't love her family, it's just that she didn't care for the drama of them very much. She was sure that other families didn't feel the way that hers did—all that pent up frustration sitting heavy between the walls until it broke out at the moment you had the least emotional energy for it. She wanted to get back to the city. She sat on the bench at Parramatta Station. The train was at least ten or fifteen minutes away. Teenagers threw hot chips onto the railroad tracks. A young mother in an oversized puff jacket pushed her child in a stroller. Clare was tired. It was the sort of day when she would spend the whole afternoon in some kind of internal fog.

On the train she picked a seat close to the window. She was ready to sit and watch places shift by through the glass. She was ready for some quiet space but she only got it until the first stop.

At Granville, Paul came down the stairs into her cabin. She looked at him and looked away but he'd already seen her seeing him. There was that awkward moment when he floated around in the aisle near her seat as if he was waiting for permission before sitting down. And then, that was it. She was stuck.

Clare didn't know where to look so she looked out the window. Still, she could feel his presence there beside her, the heat off his skin. He smelled like bread and butter pudding. She watched the industrial estates of Clyde as they appeared and disappeared through the train window. She picked at the dirt underneath her thumbnail. She noticed he was doing the same. He was the first one to speak.

'So, did you have a nice weekend?'

It took her too long to answer his question but eventually she got there. 'Yeah, just family stuff you know. My dad had a retirement party. Everyone was there. Kind of got out of hand.'

She looked out to the huge rectangles of lawns in the backyards of houses somewhere near Auburn. She liked these glimpses into the private lives of others; a man smoked, staring out at the sky, a woman hung her lingerie, a kid rode in circles on his tricycle, a horse—there was always a random horse hanging around unnoticed in someone's backyard in these neighbourhoods. And what else? Brick ovens for bread-making that reminded her of crematoriums, small alleyways between houses you could only see from the train.

'You on your way to work or you going home?' Paul asked. He sat back in his chair, cracked his knuckles. There was an easiness to him, he had a more comfortable way of being in the world than she had originally thought. She had a tendency to get so uptight about things sometimes, she had to remind herself that it was a feeling beneath her own skin. It wasn't shared by everyone else in her proximity.

She realised she had forgotten to keep the conversation going. She should have asked a question in response to his question. This is the way that conversation worked. She knew that, but she frequently forgot. Outside the sky was overcast. Perhaps it would rain soon.

'Sundays are my day off. I think I'll go do some shopping, walk home from Central.'

The truth is she imagined she just wanted to wander around the streets for a while to shake the Parramatta off her. Maybe she would see a movie on Oxford Street and buy salty liquorice to eat alone in the dark, or beg one of her teacher friends to come and have a beer with her in the afternoon.

Clare remembered she was meant to ask a question. 'Are you rostered on today?'

Paul flicked the hair out of his face by jerking his head back slightly. Up close his skin was more uneven, there was the slight scarring of acne on his cheekbones.

'No. Just going in to meet some friends.'

She noticed for the first time that he was carrying an enormous backpack like the Year Sevens she used to teach would, bags so full they were bigger than the kids carrying them. He reached into the top of his backpack and pulled out a plastic bag full of the flat bacon-and-cheese pizza rolls you buy at bakeries.

'Want one?' He put the bag down on her lap and opened the top, grabbing one for himself and leaving the rest there. They sat awkwardly on her lap feeling damp and warm against her skirt and inched slowly forward towards the seat in front. It was exactly what she wanted in her semi-hungover fog. She took one and put the bag between them. Strathfield slid past the window.

The pizza roll was just as good as it looked. 'Thanks.'

'Welcome,' he said biting into one of his own, 'I made them this morning.'

'You made them? You make your own bread?'

'You don't remember. When I was in school I used to bring you stuff from my parents' shop in Granville. I brought you

Vietnamese breakfast from their shop, hot sugared dough sticks, you remember? In the mornings. You said it was the best thing you'd ever had. I thought you would remember.'

The train stalled at Redfern. He searched her face with the one eye that wasn't covered in hair. 'Yeah,' she was starting to realise now why she looked at him and always thought—*bread*. 'I do remember now. Sorry it's just that those first few years of teaching, you know, they're kind of a blur.'

'Yeah. I know. You couldn't really cope.'

Clare wasn't expecting that. He was right, but it was still unnerving to be handed such a declaration so quietly and without malice, just like that, a clear statement of fact that was so true but so unsaid before that she felt like he had just taken her clothes off. She looked away from him. The remnants of the pizza roll were still in her hand. She shoved a too-large chunk of it into her mouth to stop whatever words might come out without her thinking.

The train pulled up at Central. It was her stop. She gathered her purse and her overnight bag up close to her chest and stood. Paul got up too, moved out into the aisle and paused a moment before walking to the front of the carriage and out through the door in front of her.

Outside it had started to storm and although there weren't so many people on the platform everyone was crowded close together in the middle to avoid the rain that was now beginning to bypass the roof and come in horizontally from the sides. Paul stood next to Clare, not moving, with his giant backpack hiked up high on his back.

'Was it that obvious?' She needed to know.

'To me it was.'

8

S o, maybe he should have stayed home after it all blew up, or maybe he should have gone home eventually, but there were better things to do and besides who ever wanted to be at home anyway?

It was the morning after the party. A Sunday and Francis was at Burger King again. Outside there was the *thump*, *thump* of a car with its bass turned up. The pop and scuttle of tires accelerating too fast over concrete. The screeching of the train on the railway line and Britney Spears screaming *I'm a slave for you* over the loudspeakers. They came here for the quiet. Not the kind of quiet that comes with no sound. The kind of quiet you find in a place where you don't need to impress anyone.

Not too long ago Francis had seen Clare walk past the front windows on her way to the station. She'd be back home by now, probably, reading fat books or writing poetry or reciting Shakespeare or whatever. He couldn't imagine it at all, really, what she did when she was alone.

Inside Burger King was full of tweens with bags of crap they bought at Westfield and goths from the nightclub next door. Tall thin white men with dirty hair entered through the front doors and ran up the back stairs and didn't come down again. It was a run-down version of a 1950s milk bar. The walls had been decorated with posters that advertised Pepsi and Lifebuoy Soap. Someone had drawn thick black texta tags over the faces of the smiling kids.

Jesús and Charbel and Francis all had cans of VB between

their legs under the table and burgers and chips up above. Charbel insisted that beer cured hangovers and Francis and Jesús just liked to drink.

'What?' Charbel said.

'I don't know. What?'

'What?'

Francis didn't say any more; that was about all he had for now. They were back to silence. Jesús picked at his chips and yawned. Francis poured a bit of VB into his waxy Burger King cup and sipped it. He picked up his Whopper and shoved it in his mouth.

Jesús had fallen asleep at the table. His arms were folded across his chest. The only way Francis could tell he wasn't dead was because of his snoring, just loud enough so that he could hear it when the kids at the table next to them stopped scream-ing. Charbel always looked so awake, as if his big round eyes might pop out of his shaved head and move across the room if he had to keep sitting there. He never seemed to get tired. He was slurping down his VB like he didn't care who was looking. He didn't look at Francis. He looked around the restaurant. He was busy surveying the scene. Francis looked beyond his head to the woman at the table behind him who was reaching into her handbag over and over again and pulling out handfuls of the odd crap women keep in their bags, lipsticks and tissues and breath mints. She dropped it all onto the surface of the table.

Charbel looked up at Francis and gave him an oversized smile. He held a couple of chips covered in tomato sauce in his fat hands in front of his face. 'So what's up with your fuckin' dad?'

Francis wasn't sure where to start answering that question, and, to be fair, the two of them had been having the 'what's up with your fuckin' dad?' talk for years. Each one of their dads was the most fucked up, depending on the time, the year, whatever they were doing to piss them off. Jesús never talked about his dad. They all knew he was probably dead. They all knew it had something to do with politics and Chile and why he had grown up here with his mum and no one else, but none of them knew how to talk about it.

And anyways, Francis was tired of this conversation. He'd had it too many times with his sister who was always calling up demanding answers, as if there was some sheet of facts he was hiding from her.

'Don't know. Same old shit I suppose. Or different shit but same shit anyways.'

'My dad says he saw your dad on CCTV throwing rocks at Lot 185.'

'Yeah, that's probably him.'

'Serious. Only didn't report it on account of you and your family and plus he feels real bad for your dad about everything that's happened but you gotta get ya dad to stop doing it, he's got enough problems, right? Doesn't need any more.'

Charbel looked at Francis, looked at him hard. Not in an aggressive way but in a way that said he meant business. It was a warning from Charbel's family to his. Sometimes Francis thought *everyone's just the same*, like in high school, where Charbel got to call all the shots because he was so loud and so confident and Francis only got to be that guy who followed him around all the time waiting for some of that slickness, that easy way of being in charge, to rub off on him a little.

'No worries. I'll just do something about that. Don't know what but somethin'. Embarrassing shit, that is.'

'What?' Jesús was suddenly awake. He licked his lips, pushed his thick black hair behind his ears, wanted to know what they were going on about.

'Francis' dad.'

'Yeah, I know. Rock-thrower. Remember how pissed he was when he had to pick us up from the police station that one time, back ages ago, when we was in school?'

Francis was hoping that Jesús would stop there and he did. He got distracted by a blonde in hot pants slinking by their table. Jesús stared at her for a while. He nodded slightly at her and smiled his boy-band smile whenever she turned slightly his way. Charbel looked at Francis and they smiled a half-smile at each other that said they both knew the other was still pissed.

Francis was glad that Jesús didn't go any further. He didn't want him to say anything to Charbel about watching his dad last night. Francis had decided not to talk about it with any-body. He and Jesús had watched it silently, and then walked on to Collectors without talking about it afterwards. And besides, they were drunk and maybe it wasn't what it looked like. After his dad had walked out of the house, his mum had turned up the music and Clare had grabbed their retarded uncle and started to dance. That's just what those two were like, but Francis couldn't stand it, all that fakeness, so he'd left too, out that same back door his father had left through, and then Jesús had followed. They'd all followed each other because none of them ever really knew what to do next.

Charbel picked his cigarettes up off the table and they fol-lowed him outside. They sat on a bench near the arcade and smoked. There were two small Chinese girls with pigtails and dresses that were too pink and had too much lace. They looked something like four and six. It made Francis dizzy, watching them passing a ball that lit up and sparkled back and forth, back and forth. He looked at Charbel, lying against the bench, surveying the scene, like he owned all the concrete he was looking at. He probably did. His family had been steadily buy-ing up the neighbourhood for years now. It was starting to get on Francis' nerves, just like it got on his father's. He couldn't say exactly why it bothered him so much.

Jesús inhaled deeply on his cigarette, leaned his arms against his thighs and let out a heap of smoke. Five feet away from them, an old woman sat on a milk crate outside a two-dollar shop like someone had washed her and set her out there to dry.

Charbel rolled up the sleeves of his thin black cotton blazer and looked at his big-arse metal watch. Francis wondered where he had been all night. Everyone he hung around, including his father, was living a kind of half-life and you never knew which half you were seeing. They kept smoking and Francis waited for both of them to say they had to piss off somewhere. Francis was always the last to leave. He had a thing about it, about staying till the end. It made him feel like he was better than everyone else in some way, like he had this kind of commitment to things, even things that meant nothing and no one else could match it.

'Gotta head,' Jesús said and Charbel nodded and looked at his watch again.

'Same.'

Charbel was probably off to have Sunday lunch with his family but he'd never admit to doing ordinary things that everyone else does. Both Jesús and Francis nodded at him, slowly, like everyone in the room knew he wasn't any more important than shit, then Jesús was off too, following not so far behind him, and Francis was left on the bench still smoking the same cigarette.

He just sat there, looking, trying to shake the fog out of his head. Francis hoped his mum wouldn't be home when he got home. He didn't want to have any kind of real conversation with anyone today. Clare would call him later. He would make a point of not answering until she'd called him for a few days in a row, and then he'd make up some kind of excuse neither of them would find believable, and everyone'd just get on with it.

For a few minutes, while he was looking, he thought he saw his dad in front of the chemist. There was a man with the same kind of navy-blue slacks and long-sleeved collared top his dad always wore outside of work. He had the same thinning grey hair on the back of his head and he was leaning against a cane, looking at the specials in the window. He knew though, knew absolutely that it wasn't his father. After watching his dad last night he knew better this new shape of his. He knew which way he leaned into his cane, how he paused for a long time before he made any moves. He'd realised, for the first time since the accident, just how different his father's body had become. Even as he got older, his father had always been such a strong man, his body shaped by many years of hard labour, he still had muscles in his arms that made the sleeves on his shirts look slightly too tight. Francis didn't know where all those muscles had gone now, they seemed to have melted back into his skin.

He didn't even know if his father knew they'd been following him the night before. They hadn't even tried to make it look like they weren't behind him. Francis and Jesús had stopped every block or so, sat on someone's fence, had a smoke, while his dad stopped and looked at a house. It had gone on like this over and over again: his dad walked slowly, looked at every house like he'd never seen it before, stopped for a little while at some, for a longer time at others, just stared and stared. Some of the places had seemed to piss him off if he looked at them too long. That's when he'd start having a conversation with no one they could see, not loud, just low and quiet like he was conspiring or maybe he was just talking to himself, who knows? And sometimes, something had pissed him off so much he'd get to destroying things. Not much, a rock thrown at a window, a paling on a wooden fence kicked until it cracked. The thing was, watching his dad, you could tell he was trying to fuck something up in a serious way but he couldn't move so fast anymore and even though the cast had been taken off his arm he couldn't really throw anything with much force, it had all just made him look kind of pathetic and that was really what made Francis feel empty—not that his dad wanted to fuck things up, but that he couldn't do it properly. That was kind of tragic in itself.

9

Early Sunday evening. The neighbourhood smelled of meat roasting over coal barbeques. Rose was standing in the back of Lucy's garden at the far left edge of the yard near where Lucy had, years ago, built a discreet gate into the fence between their houses and Antonio had, after much debate, agreed to let it stay there.

Rose watched as Lucy painted the guttering of her house in a pale blue. She had watched Lucy build her place for years, watched it grow slowly from one room to five, watched its colour palette expand from white to include the creams and blues she used now. Lucy was the only woman Rose had ever known who never got married, who used a tool-belt, who just was who she was.

Blue. Cream. White. Lucy had gotten better at things over the years. Flecks of colour no longer ended up in the blades of grass on her lawn. Antonio could no longer find as many reasons to be critical.

Rose looked at Lucy and thought that in some other life she would like to be her, or at least to inhabit her skin for a little while. They had been at some point like half-lovers, the way that women can be when they are young. They had lived together way back when they both started working at the hostel.

For two years then, they'd shared a one-bedroom flat in a brown-brick rectangle of an apartment block behind the hostel. The walls had been white, they'd had a Bunsen burner, a kettle, a couple of mattresses and chairs, Rose's prized poster of Audrey Hepburn in *Roman Holiday*. They used to go to the dance halls in Fairfield on Saturday nights and they'd hung out with Lucy's relatives at the Polish Club on Sunday afternoons. There'd been no place in the world more exciting than where they were.

Back then, Rose went shopping and ate dinner and gossiped and did everything with Lucy while she waited for a blinding and furious kind of love to arrive, like women always had in movies. She hadn't met Antonio by accident: she'd moved all the way to the outskirts of the city so that she could be found like Cary Grant found Audrey Hepburn in *Charade*.

The first time she met Antonio he was standing out in the yard of the hostel.

'Where are you from?' he asked.

Rose had watched him hold words in his mouth until he let them come out fully formed. She'd liked the sweet formality of his speech. At first she'd thought he was one of those men that meant nothing by their talk but later she'd understood that he was reserved, that living in hard places had taught him to hold things back.

But now, she watched as Lucy climbed halfway down the ladder and paused to look up at her work from another angle. After all these years, Lucy still had hair the colour of butter, still wore it in a ponytail drawn tightly at the back of her head. She wore a loose collared blouse over grey slacks and petite brown loafers. Next to her, the house looked enormous.

When she got to the bottom of the ladder she turned around and looked at Rose as if she'd expected to see her standing there all along. She gave Rose the kind of weak smile you give another person when someone they know has died, and then said, 'Right, come in.'

Rose followed her through the back door and into the kitchen where Lucy went through the same motions she always did. She got the black tray from the side of the fridge, filled a pot with tea and placed several biscuits onto a plate. Then they walked in silence from the kitchen to the front living room. Lucy still had that newspaper article sitting framed by the front door. She had pointed out the child she once was to Rose, but Rose couldn't remember her amongst those masses of children smiling and waving from the deck of the ship. What a different person Lucy might have been back then, when she was a nervous child in a new country, a resident of Villawood Migrant Hostel herself long before she had worked there.

They sat out on the plastic chairs on the small verandah where they could watch the main street. This was how it went. They needed to talk, but talking always happened outside of houses. They sipped their tea, waited, watched those women with the knee-length skirts and the handkerchiefs on their heads walk their children down to worship at the empty house down the street.

'He's gone,' Rose said, and Lucy nodded her head, shrugged her shoulders, took another sip of tea. Her gestures said *this was expected*.

On the street, a grown man rode a child's BMX past them. He looked enormous and awkward on such a small thing. His bony legs extended like chicken wings with the meat eaten off on either side. Lucy looked at the man on the bike like he might have an answer and said, 'Do you think there's something else wrong with him? You know, like, more wrong than his usual wrong?'

Lucy had never hidden the fact that she thought Antonio was slightly unhinged. It had never bothered Rose that Lucy thought this way. It just made Antonio more attractive to her. It gave him a bit more of an edge. But the kind of edge it gave him wasn't nearly as attractive in his older age. Not when you were looking forward to things finally becoming slower. Now it just made him surly and pensive the way he resisted going softly, giving in to age.

'I don't know. Retirement? It's that thing that men go through, you know, when they don't feel useful anymore.'

'Hmmm . . . ' Lucy tapped her nail against the edge of her teacup and nodded. 'But what about you? No good for you, him taking off in the middle of the night.'

Truth was, Rose still wasn't so sure where he was, but she was sure he wouldn't be that far away. These days, he just orbited the neighbourhood, he was out driving the streets or walking around the shops, or he was at one of the clubs or the library. He never invited her.

'But what am I supposed to do?' This was the question that no one seemed able to answer for her.

'Talk to him.' Lucy said it like it was that simple and then looked out to the street where the lights had just gone on and shrugged her shoulders at no one. *Talk*. They both knew Antonio wasn't that sort of man. It was probably why Lucy and he had never gotten along very well. They both were who they were, and there was no talking them out of it.

'Or you could move in with me.'

Rose had already done that a few times over the years. It always felt like going backwards. She looked away from the street and back into Lucy's house through her front window to where the television she had left on silent was beginning to throw a weak coloured light against the lounge room walls. In the corner of the room Lucy's image of the Black Madonna hung there staring at the television set. As soon as Rose forgot that Lucy had come from some different country, there it was again, same as the one that hung in the hall at the Polish Club where they had danced all those years before.

'Look, look,' she heard Lucy say, quietly, almost in a whisper. When Rose turned her head back to the street, there he was, Antonio, on the other side, walking slowly, leaning his good arm on his cane and pausing every once in a while to look off down the street. He didn't look their way, not even for a minute.

Rose watched him walk in a diagonal across the street and to their house next door, watched him search his pockets for the key, same way he'd done for the last thirty years. He finally found it and opened the door.

Lucy and Rose just sat there on those plastic chairs until the sun had set, until the neighbourhood had settled itself for the night. Across the road, the red glow of lanterns came from everywhere and nowhere. The sky was almost full up with moon. This time of year the nights were meant to be getting shorter, but it felt like the nights out here got longer all the time.

'I suppose I should go home.' It wasn't clear if Rose was asking a question or making a statement.

'Up to you,' Lucy pulled her legs up onto her chair, wrapped her arms around her knees. 'I'm going to go inside though, make some dinner, you're welcome to join.'

Really, Rose didn't want to do anything. Mostly, she'd just like to sit there and not have to make any decisions about anything ever again.

'No I suppose I should go home.'

Lucy got up, walked herself back into the house and Rose followed her through to the back garden. It was something of an unspoken habit that they both always entered and exited each other's houses through the gate in the backyard. Lucy, with one hand on Rose's back, opened the gate for her. 'You know where I am,' she said, and kissed Rose on the cheek before Rose walked through, silent and alone.

In her own backyard Rose looked at the house she had known for such a long time and thought that it looked unfamiliar. The back porch light she always kept on was off. The blue light that seeped out between the small cracks of the venetian blinds said that he was watching television.

There was the smell of overripe tomatoes in the garden. The

watermelon vines were wrapping themselves around the lettuces and choking them to death. When the heat came there would be too many flies.

When she entered through the back door he was sitting on the recliner. The back of his head just slightly above the top of the chair, his left arm hung over the side, he held a bottle of beer loosely by the neck. Rose announced her presence by letting the screen door slam shut.

He turned around as she came towards him, gave her a half smile, nodded his head.

'Where've you been?' he said, as though she were the one who was prone to wandering, as if they would have connected more lately if it weren't for their busy schedules.

10.

T he photograph of Antonio's father sat on the mantel-piece. He was standing in his orchard, his arms folded across his chest, his lips pressed together. His father was stout and serious. A man used to work. A working man's man. Next to the image, a small crumbling statue of St. Francis, the one that was meant to keep Antonio safe, always.

On the TV, the dull man. The average, ordinary type of Australian man who does not talk too loud or too soft. He said in his perfectly paced sentences: 'We will decide who comes to this country and the circumstances in which they come.'

Antonio sat back in his leather recliner and pushed the handle on the right side that made the footrest pop out. He lay back, rested his beer in his lap, watched the TV. More boats on the screen. Australians were obsessed with boats. He flipped the channel to the Italian news. What were you meant to do all day when no one wanted you to work anymore? He looked at the cracked paint in the cornices of the ceiling. He needed to sand those corners back, to rub them over with sugar soap and paint them again.

We will decide . . . We will decide . . .

He looked at that image of his father again, focused on the hills behind him. '*La miseria.*' Those mountains had been infected with the fever of departure since the beginning of time. One of those people who'd been infected with that fever was Antonio Martone. By the time Antonio had left Calabria at the age of twenty-three, he'd already been relocated north twice, after his village flooded, and that experience had shown him how easy it was to get up and go, to come back (perhaps). From the apartment he shared with his brother Christopher, he could see the famous illusions of refracted light and air that appeared in the straits sometimes, Morgan le Fay's ghost boats calling him from the land into the sea.

Christopher. He didn't have an image of his brother. Didn't want one. Christopher, the boy his mother had said was 'no good from the start', who always smelled like whisky and the cold damp of the mountain air. The year Antonio left, Christopher was twenty-seven and should have been married already, but instead he had a scar on his cheek that told the story of him getting up to no good.

The night before he'd left home, Antonio, in his mother's absence, had cut tomatoes and heavy slices of bread for their dinner, and brought in rainwater he'd caught on their balcony when the taps stopped working for weeks on end.

'Where do you go all day?' he used to ask Christopher, but he never got any answers.

Antonio didn't really want to know, not exactly, not any more than he'd wanted to know the exact details of what happened to his parents' bodies when their house was eaten by a river of mud rushing down the mountain.

Here in his living room, the man on the TV was saying the same thing over and over again. 'We will decide who comes to this country, and the circumstances in which they come.' He should get up and close the window. He could see particles of dust floating in the lamplight. Next door they were building a block of apartments. As soon as Mrs. Tsilimidis had died her kids had sold off her house to developers. They wanted his house too. But Antonio wasn't selling anything.

He thought of Christopher again, sitting at the table of the apartment they'd shared, tearing at a thick slice of bread with his teeth. To Antonio, their father's face was imprinted on Christopher—a ghost sitting just underneath his skin. It had been like that the last time Antonio had spoken to his father—he'd sat at the kitchen table watching him biting chunks out of something with his oversized jaws. His father was a big man too, like Christopher, but he always looked smaller, softer. There wasn't the hardness around his jaw. That last time, he had tried to explain how it was, how because Christopher was the eldest he would get the land, because, he said, 'That's how it is.' But the tone he'd said it in had made it clear he'd wished it was some other way and Antonio had wanted to say that it was all right, that he understood. Forgave him, even, for the way he turned away when Christopher struck Antonio with his fists, for the way he was so strong but too slow to run that last time the floods had come down the mountain. There must have been other conversations after that, but in his mind that was the last time they spoke.

As he looked around, he thought his father would be proud of this place. Antonio had built his home with his own bare hands. His bare hands. People just didn't appreciate that anymore. Buy a block.

Knock everything down. Turn it into apartments with walls made of pressed cardboard. Nico and he had built their houses at the same time. Nico had built in Villawood but Antonio wanted out, wanted to get as far away as he could, so he'd landed in Parramatta, before all the apartments went up. This living room used to be the kitchen. The garage used to be the living room. That's the way it was, you built one room at a time, you lived in one room until you could afford another. You used the best materials you could find.

The facade of his house had even been made of real sandstone. Nico had helped him get it cheap from a developer who had been clearing a gravesite to build houses. They'd sat four weekends in a row on Antonio's front lawn chiselling the headstones into squares to cement onto the wall. If you picked your way through the interior walls of his house until you hit the back of that sandstone you'd find names there. 'Mrs. Jane Smiley 1890–1940, May She Rest in Peace', something like that over and over again. He liked the way it gave the place a history that was longer than itself, as if all those people were watching over him.

Back then he and Nico had been working at the Vandyke Housing Factory during the week and building their own homes all weekend. The power of the machines amazed him every time. One careless move and a bandsaw could cut your arm off in three seconds flat. Slicing through wood and fibro-cement board, they knocked out houses quicker than his father could harvest an olive tree. That was the way things were back then, standing next to Nico in his loudness and largeness, feeding planks through sanding machines, after the war, in a new country, making new houses.

Nico had arranged that job for him too, and for all the other Calabrians at the hostel. When he'd shown up at the factory he'd had to tell Mr. Van Dyke that he'd been 'doing this sort of work for years in the old country'. Nico told him not to mention that he grew up farming olives or that he'd never seen a factory before.

Who comes to this country?

Outside, that new apartment building was going up. The noise of it. They were using a concrete hammer with the wrong-sized bit on the shaft. He could hear it in the thump and halt of the metal hitting the ground. *We have the right . . .* He turned the television off. He didn't want it on anymore. He adjusted his chair.

That image of his father on the mantelpiece undid him sometimes. He thought of him carrying old metal oil drums half filled with olives up and down the hills of his childhood. Calabria was so dry in summer, so very wet in winter. In those winter months the dry, still earth suddenly got up and moved as though it had been waiting for this moment all year to shake off its dormancy and show the world what it could do. The rain came and then it came some more. Sheets and rivers and days of rain. The whole place turned to mud and smelled of shit. At this time, post-World War II, the earth was already unstable on account of being blown to pieces by the allied forces not so long before. The pockmarked places on the side of the mountain where those bombs had hit filled with water and turned to mud. The buildings too, they turned to mud and the weak frames of houses that had been built too high, to fit too many people, they became bloated and collapsed and the people went with them, hit by falling debris, like his parents, they floated, unconscious, in the houses that became their tombs.

Whole villages had vanished like that. The lucky ones survived, moved, materialised again somewhere else. Antonio still remembered that woman, back in the big flood of '53, remembered her face more than he remembered his own mother's; the blue of her twisted dress above her knees, the dirt caught in the lines around her eyes, her open mouth, the soft peachy lips, the way her limp arms hung around the base of a tree in his parents' orchard. He saw the woman in the blue dress everywhere that winter: she was the woman screaming for her son in the main street, she was the woman who jumped the bread queue, she was the reflection in the window from his parents' house, the remnants of which he'd found in the dirt at the base of the mountain.

The circumstances
in which
they come

11.

Maybe it was the sex. Maybe it wasn't. She had always thought that sex might be able to give her more of a physical presence that she could feel, as though it could switch something on inside of her so she could stop feeling as though she was never fully awake. She wanted it to bring her back into her own body, to connect her in a sharp, focused way to the world. Clare had always thought that she would find sex less boring if she found the right person to do it with in the right way. After she went through that phase of letting herself get picked up at The Clock most Saturday nights, she realised it wasn't true. Even in books, sex was boring or at best laughable—no matter what the author intended or the character said it felt like. But at least it wasn't messy; at least you could turn the page and not worry about cleaning up afterwards.

And then there was Richard. He was an old sometimes-habit like chewing your nails. Richard sat up in her bed, stretched his arms over his head. His back was long and freckled and the bones stuck out from his thin frame. Clare watched him slide his hand from the top of his skull to the base of his neck. He was looking away from her and at the wall where she had a poster of Ernest Hemingway reading in bed.

'Hemingway,' Richard said to no one but himself, reading the word out slowly from its lettering at the bottom of the poster.

Clare scooped her shirt off the floor with her right hand without even looking down and pulled it over her head.

'Always do sober what you said you'd do drunk.'

'What?'

'Hemingway. It's Hemingway's famous line. "Always do sober what you said you'd do drunk".'

'Ah,' he smiled a half-smile, scratched his belly softly. This was the point at which she wanted him to leave. She wanted him to get out of her bed and put on the crumpled pair of jeans she could see sitting behind her bedroom door where he had left them in his own efficient way, taking them off before he'd even touched her, before he'd even made it to the bed.

Clare stood up, put on the faded pink pyjama pants her mother had given her so long ago, tied her hair back in a pony-tail. Downstairs she could hear her housemates yelling at a sporting match on the television. In her grandmother's old mirror hanging on the wall, she looked at the bags under her eyes and wondered if she was too old for share houses. Thirty. She was thirty now. She wondered when she would start to feel like an adult.

What she would like to do, really, was spend the rest of the evening reading in bed. She wanted to fall asleep with a book by her side and get up again tomorrow morning and read it some more and now that she'd had sex with Richard she could do these things and stop feeling like she hadn't put some kind of effort into the outside world. This evening though, he was in a slow mood. He didn't look like he'd be going anywhere anytime soon. He moved the sock he had abandoned on the ground around with his right foot. Clare sat down next to him on the bed. She folded her hands in her lap. Yawned.

'What are you doing tonight?'

She knew what he was doing tonight. She just couldn't think of anything else to say. He was going to see a documentary about pineapple farmers in a place that was hot and far away.

'Going to see a film. You can come, if you want.' Finally he picked up his socks, looked at them, put them on, began to make a move.

She didn't want to go. He didn't really want her to go. They both knew these things. Back when they were at uni, they'd hung out together more, but that was when they were young enough not to care that they didn't have much to say to each other. When they were younger, it had been enough just to be together and to drink cheap beer and to ask someone you didn't have much in common with endless questions about their life. Now that they were older, time was more important, even if they just spent it by themselves. They didn't have the time to hang out with people just for the sake of it, so they didn't do outside spaces together. He crossed the room and put on his jeans and his old Led Zeppelin shirt. She watched him put his red Vans on. He hardly looked down, just slipped his feet into them, used her dresser to steady himself with his right hand before tightening a shoelace with his left.

Clare made her bed, as if she wasn't going to get right back into it when he left. When he was finished getting dressed and she was sitting on the bed he came and sat beside her like he always did. He put his arm around her shoulder, rubbed it and said, 'Was that alright?' She hated the way he asked this every time. Her friend Hannah reckoned he did this because, like most men, he needed his ego stroked, but Clare knew that this wasn't entirely true, not in Richard's case anyway. Even having sex he wanted to make sure he went about it with the right politics.

'Yep, fine.' It was the question, not the sex, that made her blush. He was always so conscious of being good, of making the right decisions and doing the right things by people. She couldn't arouse in herself that same kind of consciousness. It wasn't that she didn't care, but that she just couldn't remember to think about everyone and everything all the time in the same way that he did. She yawned, smiled at him, hoped he got the hint.

'I'll walk you downstairs.'

'Sure.'

In the hallway there was the musty smell that these old terraces have. Her housemate, Anita, had left one of her orange platform pumps on the ground outside her bedroom door. The new housemate, Greg, a postgrad student from the UK, had put a poster of Derrida up on the wall. It was the kind of place that made her feel interesting. That's why she lived here. She suspected that's why most people lived in Surry Hills— because it made them feel interesting.

Richard went before her, took two or three steps at a time, like he always did, almost jumping. In the living room at the bottom of the stairs the television was up too loud. It was a football game that Greg was watching, his face was in his hands, some team he had sworn his allegiances to was losing. He looked up for a moment, stared at Richard and said, 'They're smashing us.'

Richard nodded his head sympathetically, made a kind of half-arsed gesture of looking at the TV as if he cared about what was on it and shrugged his shoulders. Greg looked over his shoulder momentarily, past Richard and towards Clare, gave her a half smile that made her wonder if he was judging her or just curious.

She turned away from him and walked with Richard to her front door. Richard kissed her on the cheek, let himself out and she stood against the doorframe for a while just watching the street. The nights were beginning to warm up again but the people hadn't started coming out of their houses yet. It was quiet this time of evening, right after everyone had made their way home from work and too early for anyone to be on their way out again. It was twenty to six and she had the feeling that in all these terraces, people were getting ready for something big to happen. She was going to make herself toast with plenty of butter and get back into bed with a bottle of wine and a glass and E.M. Forster or John Cheever or maybe Virginia Woolf.

When she turned around she saw that Richard had left his cap in the hallway. Perhaps she wouldn't call him again. It was just that it was Monday night and she needed something to help her get over the horror of the weekend at her parents' place. At least Richard helped to remind her that she wasn't under her father's roof anymore.

12

Monday. Nothing else to do and Lucy was at his house again taking up all his space. That Filipina woman who made coffee pushed a heavy plastic chair from the café all the way to the TAB section of the Parramatta RSL because she saw him struggling to sit on a stool with his cane. He sat there out of politeness, but now he wished he hadn't. He was sitting with his head angled way back like a child trying to catch what he could of the three screens on the wall, looking up between the bodies of the men on their stools.

He wanted a beer but he didn't want to look even more ridiculous than he already was, sitting in a chair made for people having tea and finger sandwiches. The men looked like they had been here all their lives. They moved over slightly when someone new sat down, knowing exactly where he would take his place on the table. They talked without speaking in the way that men do, through gestures and a nod of the head.

Antonio folded the form guide in his lap, looked at the TV, folded the guide again in a different way. There weren't as many people to talk to now that he wasn't on site all day. It wasn't exactly that he didn't want to talk to Rose; it was more that he couldn't find enough to say to her when they were together so much. He didn't have any news from his day out in the world to give her; there was nothing to report back, and now she was always trying to get him to talk about his feelings. He'd even found a book she bought hidden behind the couch,

Getting Your Man to Open Up. He was no one's man. No one's.
Not even his wife's. It wasn't that he didn't want to talk; he just
didn't want to talk about things that were bullshit. He wanted
his son to tell him what the men were saying about him on the
site. He wanted his daughter to talk to him like he wasn't some
kind of invalid. He wanted the guys he used to work with to
come over more often and have a beer and not talk about
much. There were more interesting things going on in the
world than his own feelings.

He got himself up. Wobbled slightly. Hoped that no one
saw. At the bar he ordered himself a beer. Next to him, he
thought for a minute that he saw Charbel.

'Hey . . . ' he began to say, but when the other guy turned
around fully he saw that it was some other young bloke, but
now, anyway, they'd caught each other's eye.

'You here to see Philip Ruddock?' He smiled that kind of
big enthusiastic smile that you only see in children and politicians. Antonio looked at the other smiling face on his shirt and
the words beneath: Ross Cameron 2001.

He had seen the posters on the way in. Hadn't paid that
much attention. There were people's disembodied heads smiling everywhere now that it was election time. He could see
behind this young man that there were others filing in wearing
Ross Cameron shirts. An older guy, somewhere around his age,
with cheeks that looked like grey sandpaper came up to the bar
and ordered a beer.

'Yeah,' Antonio said. 'I'm going.' Why not? There was
nothing else to do but sit in that big ridiculous chair.

'Cheers then,' the young man said, raising his glass and
clicking it against Antonio's.

He followed the young bloke to the back room of the RSL
where the rows of plastic chairs were already filling up. The
young man shook his hand and patted him on the back before
walking away, as if he'd already done something great just by

being there, just by being him. Someone had tied bundles of blue and white balloons to the legs of the table next to him. He looked at the brochures on the table. 'Population Control', 'The Chinese Welfare Society', 'Our Fragile Soils', 'Protecting the Border', 'Family Fun Day'. He'd been in this room a few times on Rose's insistence. At night it was filled up with retirees who danced in too-tight skirts and polyester pants to music they'd loved when they'd still been young enough to get away with their outfits.

A set of scales was projected onto the screen at the front of the room. One side of the scales held the words 'humanitarian intake' and 'skilled migration' while the other side held the words 'social integration' and 'economic impact'. At the top of the screen the word 'balance' floated around in space. At the side of the stage there were two men with blank faces that lacked, completely, any sign of emotion. One of them moved forward to the centre of the stage, coughed, tapped the microphone. The audience went silent.

'I'm honoured to introduce Philip Ruddock today who has come back home, really, to the place where his political career began in the seat of Parramatta. Phil is well known as a man of ability and compassion with a long record in the human rights field. He's here today in this community consultation to talk to us about something I know we've been hearing a lot about in the news lately, something that I know has always been of great concern to this great country with its large borders and its fragile ecosystem and may I say this great, and particularly in Parramatta, this great multicultural nation as well. But it's all about balance and that's what Phil is here to talk to us about today and that is achieving balance in migration.'

When Philip Ruddock got up he stood in front of a screen. His speech was more about lines than about scales. There was a red line with an alarming upward arc, a blue line that dipped depressingly down and a green line in the middle that edged up surely and steadily from one side of the screen to the other. Only his lips moved when he talked about his lines. There was no expression on his face at all, but somehow he still managed to let you know just how much these lines meant to him, that he had dedicated his life to making sure *that* green line went along at just the right angle and at just the right speed. 'What we want,' he said, 'what the ordinary everyday Australian wants to see is for us to achieve that green line.'

The green line. Antonio was a man that understood about lines. At night, when he navigated the streets, he thought about the places that had shaped him as different patterns of lines: the erratic contours of the hills in Calabria, the straight, straight rows of Nissen huts at the Villawood Migrant Hostel, the squares within squares of the family home he had built, the loops of the Radburn projects where he'd first worked as a builder, the concentric circles of the Macquarie Links Estate where it all ended.

When he stopped thinking lines and shapes he was back in the room again. The talking had ended. People clapped. The woman sitting next to him with the tight white bun of hair said 'marvellous, marvellous' over and over again and Philip Ruddock walked around the room shaking hands.

Antonio looked at a brochure, 'Australia's Migrant Waves: are we keeping our heads above water?' He was still looking at the glossy image of the ocean on the front cover when the grey arm of a suit extended itself out beside him and touched his shoulder firmly. 'Thank you for coming, sir.'

'No. Thank you.' Antonio looked him straight in the eyes but the man didn't flinch. Not a single part of his face moved. Not a millimetre. Here he was, this serious man and he was shaking Antonio's hand and calling him *sir*, like he was some-one to respect.

Outside the RSL, the Flame of Remembrance was about level with the sun. Antonio leaned against his cane and smoked. Three o'clock and he didn't want to walk home just yet. Two boys walked past him with their Arthur Phillip High shirts untucked. Between them they kicked a can back and forth. It had been a long time, a couple of years in fact, since Antonio had visited Clare at that school. She would be finishing now with her classes, getting ready for tomorrow. Maybe those boys were from Clare's class. He picked a few gardenias from the bush at the entrance to the RSL. Something about the lecture had made him feel a little more cheerful. Optimistic, in fact. He would go and visit Clare at work. He would refrain from commenting on her messy table. He was proud of what she did, though he rarely told her so. Unlike her brother, she'd been good from the start. A man has a boy and you expect him to grow in your image, but Francis had always been more of a mystery to him than Clare. Francis was always rebelling against something or someone, mostly Antonio, though he could never work out why.

When he got to the intersection where the school was, there was hardly room to cross the road. It was amazing to him what these kids got away with. There was an Islander boy with a bright pink hairbrush stuck in his tight curly hair and pants that were torn at the knees. He was holding hands with a blonde girl with purple streaks and a skirt that was pulled up so far it barely passed the line of her underwear. Crossing the intersection was like being stuck in a train station in Calcutta, the mob of bodies came at him from the opposite side of the road screeching loudly, whacking at each other. A boy pushed another boy and that boy slammed into Antonio's side knocking the cane out of his hand.

He fell onto the road and scraped his arm, curled up like a ball so he wouldn't get trampled. He looked up and watched the boy who had pushed him over run after a smaller boy and

push him to the ground. 'Excuse you!' Antonio said loudly to
the bunch of scuffed black shoes that walked by him.

'Excuuuuuuuuse you!' he heard someone in the crowd par-
rot back in a high-pitched squeal. Two African girls came to his
rescue. Thin things that didn't look any older than twelve.
They leaned down over him and grabbed his arms, pulling him
up without asking his permission first.

'You're going to get hit by a car, man,' one of them said as
if she was used to clearing bodies from the pavement. He
pulled his good arm back away from them and used it to prop
himself up again. Someone passed him his cane and he turned
towards the crowd that was walking away and yelled, 'You
should learn some manners!' But they didn't care what he had
to say. They were all already across the street, taking over the
convenience store.

At the school gates he caught his breath, leaned against the
bars just down from the entrance and watched the rest of them
shove their bodies out of the gate and onto the street. He wondered what the parents thought of their children. Those
Catholic schools he'd sent his kids to were worth every penny.
They made the boys get a short back and sides and the girls
wear their skirts down to their knees. He'd been devastated
when Francis ended up here. Francis had grown his hair to his
shoulders just because he could. He wondered if the parents of
these children knew what they looked like when they went to
school, or if they pulled their skirts down and brushed their
hair before they went home.

When the bodies coming out of the gates slowed down to
a trickle Antonio went inside. He knew where Clare's office
was, down the hallway and to the right. When he reached the
door it was closed. The sign said English/History Staff Room.
Underneath the sign there were posters and pictures thumb-
tacked to the door. 'Those who don't know history are
doomed to repeat it!' one sign said. Beneath it there was a

poem by a man named T.S. Eliot, also pinned to the door. Antonio remembered Clare reading his poems when she was in university. She brought them home to him and read them out loud. They were all about damaged people, crumbling societies, people who did bad things to one another. That's when Clare was hanging out with those idiotic Socialists and he'd tried to explain to her that that's where Fascism had started, and did she know that Mussolini was in the Socialist Party when he first began his career as a politician, and did she know what he did to people, to *his own* people? But Clare didn't understand because she was brought up in a country where people could always eat meat. And then there was no more T.S. Eliot and Clare didn't speak to him for a while. He read the poem to himself . . . the hollow men . . . the stuffed men.

He knocked on the door. A woman answered. She had a half-eaten sandwich in her hand and the rest of it clearly in her mouth by the way that she was chewing. She stared at Antonio. Swallowed. She wasn't one of the teachers he recognised.

'Can I help you?'

He peered into the room where another two women were hunched over computers and a man was throwing a plastic ball into a small basketball hoop that was affixed to the wall.

'I'm looking for my daughter, Clare.'

'What year is she in?'

'No. She's not a student. She's an English teacher. This is her office.'

A blank stare. 'We don't have any English teachers here named Clare.'

'Yes you do. Clare Martone? Maybe I have the wrong office.'

The man shooting the plastic ball into his hoop stopped, looked at Antonio.

'Oh, Mr. Martone. I remember you. Clare's dad.'

'Yes, Clare. I just thought I would come to see her.' Antonio looked at the gardenias in his hand. Everyone else looked at him.

'Oh, Clare. *That* Clare.' The woman said and turned to the man.

'She's not here,' the man said.

'Not here.'

That Clare. The man got up off his chair. The woman with the sandwich turned around to the two people who were looking up from their computers now. They all looked at each other like they didn't know what to do.

The man walked towards him, awkwardly, shoved his hands in his pockets.

'She doesn't work here anymore. She left about a year ago.'

'A year ago?'

The man said it to him again slowly like he might not have understood the first time. 'She doesn't work here anymore.'

'She doesn't work here? Why?'

Everyone in the room had stopped what they were doing. They searched each other's faces for the answer to the question.

'Because she doesn't. She doesn't work here anymore. You'll have to talk to her about it.' He smiled a weak smile and kept standing there, looking at Antonio.

Antonio turned and walked into the hallway. He felt the weight of something pressing against his chest. A memory interrupted his exit from the school: Clare with her pigtails in plaits, standing with a piece of chalk at the blackboard he'd given her for her twelfth birthday, writing down words for a five-year-old Francis to copy onto a sheet of paper.

He wondered who his children were now. This was the hardest thing about being a parent, the thing that no one tells you about. The fact that you grieve for your children from the moment they are born. Not so much because you've lost them but because they are always changing and you can't get back all those different versions of what they once were.

13.

Rose was conducting a raid on the garden while Antonio took a nap. The tomatoes were infected with something that made their thin red skins explode and pour out a brownish-red goo every time she came near them. The basil leaves were pockmarked brown with the scars of whatever had been eating away at them. The pumpkins had taken over everything, had marked their territory by wrapping their long green tendrils around the zucchinis and rows of beans. There were pumpkins everywhere: they'd been eating pumpkin soup and pumpkin mash and pumpkin tarts for the last three weeks. She'd even learned how to make an American pumpkin pie from a recipe she'd found in a book at the library. She couldn't imagine what else she could possibly make with a pumpkin.

In her hand she held a contraband chemical spray to get rid of the insects. Antonio favoured sprays of garlic and lemon but Rose liked the certainty of chemicals. He didn't like her messing in his yard, but they both knew he wasn't up to it now. It was impossible for him to bend over and pull out the weeds that grew between the rows of his vegetables. She spotted a weed. Bent over and pulled it out, sprayed the patch of ground with weed killer so she wouldn't need to pull out another weed in its place sometime later.

Last week she'd been caught out, though he hadn't mentioned it to her. She'd dug deep into the ground near where he'd planted wooden poles to support his eggplants. She'd found a square of plaster and dug deeper around it and pulled out the thing that was stuck in the ground there, an old statue of St. Francis he'd buried upside down when they'd first moved in, some tradition he had in Calabria about burying saints in the ground upside down to keep your house safe. Its face had been worn away. Chips of blue on the arms said it was painted once, but it looked grim in her hands, as though it had been chewed on by something underground that hadn't liked its presence there. She'd thrown it in the garbage bin but Antonio had found it somehow and it was now sitting on the mantelpiece in the living room. Neither of them had said anything to the other about it. It just sat there like a warning: *don't go near my garden.*

Antonio kept all that cultural stuff to himself. When the kids had come home from school with those assignments where they had to write about their family, he'd refused to tell them anything about his life before coming here. Clare had made a collage of images of Italy for multicultural day at her school once, and he'd just stared blankly at it and said, 'We're Australian. I'm Australian'.

Rose did know some of the story though. He'd been more willing to talk about it in the earlier days when Nico was around, helping them build their house. She remembered the two of them in the front yard with all those old tombstones, sanding them down to build the front facade of the house. They had done the heavy work and she and Mona would sweep all the dust away and bring them endless snacks and drinks. Antonio and Nico would talk about the houses in the mountains in Calabria and the way that families would just whack up another level on their house when kids got married and brought their families home, and then the war, and the floods when those houses had just fallen apart, slid down the mountain and collapsed with all the people inside them. She knew that's how Antonio had lost his parents.

'I married a peasant,' Mona used to say. She had come from Florence where the houses were solid and built on flat ground. Antonio hadn't wanted to talk about it so much since they'd had children. It was as though he didn't want to leave them with that legacy, or maybe Rose had just stopped asking him about it, she wasn't sure. Time passes, stories get lost. Then again, maybe it was just because she didn't feel like she was a part of it, maybe that's why she didn't talk about it so much. Even at her age. She'd never left Australia and here she was, surrounded by people who knew so much about the rest of the world. It made her feel small.

'Rose, Rose . . . ' She could hear him calling, probably from the same chair in the living room where he had fallen asleep two hours earlier. 'Rose, Rose . . . '

She stashed her gardening gloves and the chemicals in the shed. Inside the house the air felt heavy. It was getting heavier every day, weighing on her like she was trying to breathe through fabric. In the living room Antonio looked up, startled, like he'd already forgotten he'd called out for her. His fingers stumbled over the mechanism on the side of the chair that made the footstool drop back down again.

'Yes?'

'Where is Francis?'

He looked at her panicked, like he'd just had a bad dream. She looked at her watch, it was six. 'He's not home from work yet. Probably gone out with his mates.'

'Right.' But it wasn't.

Nothing had been right since he'd returned this afternoon—well, he'd been even more off than usual. Antonio had told Rose that Clare had quit her job at the school and she'd asked if he might have become a bit confused. He'd told her that he went to Clare's school after the RSL and all the teachers were saying she hadn't been there for a year. Then Antonio had told her that he'd been run over by a giant boy with a pink comb in his hair and girl whose skirt was above her underwear. Rose had told him that he must have fallen asleep again at the TAB and Antonio had told her about some man and all his important lines on a screen and she'd said that he needed a nap. Sometimes she just didn't want to talk to him at all. The effort was too exhausting. They went around and around and ended up at the same point.

'Where is Francis?' Antonio kept saying. 'He's never around very much.'

'He's twenty-three. He does what twenty-three-year-olds do—they hang out with their mates. He doesn't want to be at home.' She didn't really want to be at home either.

Antonio had fallen asleep with the *Sydney Morning Herald* and the *Parramatta Sun* in his lap. They fell to the floor as he got his footrest down. He had taken to reading the newspapers lately with a religious fervour, every page. There was a neat stack of them piling up in the corner of their living room. Rose watched as he folded and unfolded the *Parramatta Sun* in his lap.

'I just don't know what those kids are doing anymore.' He slouched further back in his chair. It was like his increasing lack of control over the world was hollowing out his body.

She sat down on the couch, slipped her shoes off.

'I don't know. You never know, do you, what your kids are really doing?'

Rose understood Antonio was one of those parents who used to feel sure that he knew what his kids were doing at every second of the day, but she was never under any such illusion. Everyone had their secret lives. Especially your own children.

She changed the topic.

'Maybe you should get a hobby? There's a hobby shop on Church Street. They have ships you can put together out of a model kit or you could brew your own beer or learn another language or maybe you could do some volunteer work or take up cards. They have bridge at the RSL. George likes bridge, you could go with him. You know, George across the road.'

She watched him shove his hands down the side of the couch and pull out the remote for the television. Since the party all his old friends had stayed away. She wondered if they would come back. She could never be enough to Antonio to fill a gap as large as they filled in Antonio's life. She'd learned that when she had married him. She'd tried to reorganise their lives so that they wouldn't need anyone but each other. It never worked.

Antonio switched on the news. That was his answer to her suggestions. She wondered sometimes why she even tried. She leaned back further into the couch. There was the casserole on the counter that needed to be heated up, but the effort of walking into the kitchen, of heating it up, of serving it to him on a plate, seemed like far too much for her at that moment.

Antonio fumbled with the remote, changed to another news station.

'You tell me when he gets home.'

'George?'

'Francis.'

Rose was so tired.

A map of the world popped up on a screen behind the news reporter. He showed the audience where all the places he'd been talking about were. 'There is Christmas Island, there is Indonesia, there is Nauru, there is Australia.' They were talking about turning all those boats around and sending the people on them to camps on islands where there was no water to drink and the ground was crumbling into the sea.

Not on the news: something about her husband had shifted. He was beginning to crack some time ago but now he was splitting wide open. She watched him sitting there, staring at those newspapers on his lap. He was saying something to himself. Rose could tell it was some kind of argument he was having, maybe with someone only he could see. *There's just too many of them*, he was mumbling to himself, *and now we've lost Francis and Clare.*

14.

Antonio woke up. He was lying on his recliner. The newspapers were still in his lap but the lights were off and the television was off and the only reason he could see anything at all was because of the moonlight coming in through the window and the digital clock on the VCR that threw red light onto the space in front of it. 11:30. Last thing he remembered was Rose bringing him a beer and a painkiller after dinner. He turned on the lamp beside him and looked at the double-edged quality of the room, the way the television seemed to have a fuzzy second image of a television existing behind it and slightly to the right. It was like being outside of the room and looking back at it through a distorted glass window.

He pushed himself up slowly with his good arm, found his cane next to his chair and he was up and off. He wasn't quite sure where but he needed to go. He needed to get out of this room and his own fuzzy head. His leg hurt, his arm hurt, his head hurt. He walked into the kitchen and got his packet of painkillers from the pantry above the fridge. He put one on his tongue, opened the fridge and pulled out a beer to swallow it with.

He walked through the kitchen and out to the back porch where the breeze hit his face and the air smelled like overripe tomatoes and something burning. He couldn't stand any longer.

He sat down on one of the chairs they kept there. In the far right-hand corner of the yard he could see wispy clouds of smoke rising up from behind his lattice of beans and disappearing into the sky. Lately, in the evenings, Antonio was not so sure if he really saw what he thought he saw. He put his hand into his pocket and fumbled around in his crushed pack for a cigarette, pulled one out, lit it. He inhaled deeply and looked at the far corner of the yard again where he was beginning to understand that the small clouds of smoke behind his beans were attached to a figure sitting on the ground there smoking something. It was probably Francis, but he couldn't be sure from here. It was one of those rare shared desires between him and his son, a smoke outside and a quiet moment to look at the world.

Then again, if it was Francis he should be slightly more civilised about it, should sit out on the porch like his father (with his father), not out there in the dirt. But that's just the kind of thing Francis did. Sitting in chairs was too sensible.

'Oy!' It was all Antonio could think of to say. He yelled from the porch again, 'Oy!' and saw something rustle there and jump up and turn around. It was definitely Francis. He stood up straight, dropped something he was holding in one hand and waved with the other.

This was where he was, the son he never saw even though they lived in the same house and worked on the same building sites. Perhaps this was where he was always getting to. Francis was like a weedy shirtless garden gnome with unruly hair. He was kicking something in the dirt and fumbling with his pyjama pants until he produced a cigarette, lit it and moved forward slowly towards where his father was standing on the porch.

'Couldn't sleep,' he said, stopping three feet in front of Antonio. Even though Francis was twenty-three and even though Antonio might not be as sharp as he once was, he still knew his son was up to something. But at least he'd found him here, miraculously, in his garden.

He wanted to talk to Francis like men talk to men but it was hard to talk to him in that way. How do you talk to your children when suddenly they are adults and still they are *your* children? Antonio's father was much better at these things. He always talked to Antonio and his brother like they were equals.

'Sit.' Antonio whacked his cane against the other chair on the porch.

'I got to go to bed.'

'You're up. I'm up. Sit.' Under the back porch light Antonio could see that his son's eyes were bloodshot. He wondered if Francis had been crying. He searched his face. His son had the same square jaw, high cheekbones, dark set eyes as him. They were unmistakably related. Clare looked much more like Rose.

Francis pulled the other chair further away from Antonio and sat down, putting one hand under his leg and using the other to hold his cigarette. Both of his hands were shaking, Antonio could see it, even from here, even in the dark. It worried him. He wondered how much longer someone with hands that shake like that could be a builder. Francis smelled like sweet burning cut grass. His eyes said he had been off somewhere in another kind of universe and was trying to pull himself back to the present, here with his father on the porch. Antonio had seen him like this before.

'Have you been smoking the marijuana again?'

'*Have you been smoking the marijuana again?*' Francis repeated his words in a high-pitched tone and laughed. 'You're the only one who says it like that, Dad—"smoking the marijuana".'

Antonio does not understand what he has said wrong. He was trying not to react, trying to remain calm. Francis wasn't ten anymore. He couldn't put him over his knee.

'What is wrong with you?'

'Aw, Dad, shit, don't start. Not now, not tonight.'

'I'm not trying to start anything. I am trying to have a conversation.'

'No you're not. You're just trying to get on my back . . . '

'No. I want to talk to you. I want to be able to talk to you.'

It was true. That was all he was looking for, just the ability to connect with his son. That was it. He was willing to put aside the smoking the marijuana thing, or however you said it.

'I want to be able to have a conversation with you.' He could hear himself now, that kind of begging quality in his own voice.

Francis stubbed his cigarette out on the porch, reached up to his face and rubbed his eyes with his palms.

'What then, *what*, what do you want to have a conversation about?'

Antonio didn't actually know. 'About anything. What are you doing?'

'Nothing. I'm not doing anything. Just trying to think. I can't sleep. I was just out in the garden.'

He watched his son slouch in his chair. Francis' body language made it clear that simply having a conversation was far too much effort to require of him. 'Why can't you sleep?'

'I don't know, Dad,' he let out a giant sigh. 'Why can't *you* sleep?'

'I don't know, lots of things I've been thinking about. Did you know your sister doesn't work at Arthur Phillip anymore?'

'No. Where is she working now?'

'I don't know. Do you know?'

'No. Probably a good thing though.'

'Why?'

'Because. Because it never really worked for her.'

'Why?'

'Because, Dad, just because, ask her.'

Francis holds his hands up to his face and shakes his head from side to side in his cupped hands.

'Because why?'

'Because, just because. Ask her. I'm going to bed.' Francis got up and left before his father could respond. Antonio wondered what he had said wrong this time. Why did everyone make him feel like he was always asking the wrong questions? Because, because, why. His head was too heavy, he couldn't work it out. Things didn't make sense anymore.

He heard a door slam somewhere in the back of the house. The moonlight was bright tonight and he could see all the shapes there in his garden—the tomatoes and beans on their wooden sticks, the hessian bags he had covered the pawpaws with so that birds couldn't eat them—but when he tried to make out the specifics of things they still had that double-edged quality. He pushed himself up off his chair, leaned against his cane and walked out into his garden.

He needed to get out here more. To push everything back into the neat rows they once were in. Everything was disordered, the pumpkins were in the zucchinis, in the eggplants, the tomatoes.

He walked to the row of beans where Francis had been sitting and found a small tin pencil case lying on the ground, half covered in dirt. He leaned over carefully, pulled it out of the ground, flipped open the lid. Inside there was a small lump of green and two roll-your-own cigarettes already made up. He flipped the lid closed and looked back at his house.

On the left side of the house the sensor lights had turned on again. He'd installed them only recently, but they never seemed to switch off. They were always on, sensing things when there was nothing there. He walked up towards them slowly, and when he got there, there was nothing, as usual—only the cans of blue paint that he intended to use to repaint the window frames. He kept walking towards the front of the house. The concrete slab he'd laid there all those years before was firm and cold underneath his feet and he realised for the first time that he'd forgotten to put on shoes. He sat on the park bench Rose had bought second-hand and insisted that they put there, underneath the front window. He had allowed her this one concession, and also the pots of gardenias that she'd placed on each side of it. The rest of the front yard was neat, concrete, clean.

He opened up the tin pencil case again, pulled out one of Francis' thin cigarettes and held it to his nose. It had the cut grass smell that was stuck to Francis' clothes.

'This is the marijuana,' he said out loud. When Francis had been kicked out of school for smoking it behind the school oval he'd launched into an argument with Antonio about how it was natural, better for you than the cigarettes or the beer his father was into. His children were always arguing with him, arguing from the moment they were born. Antonio couldn't remember ever fighting with his father.

He put it in his mouth, lit up, inhaled. It was harder on his throat than a cigarette. He coughed, inhaled again, got the hang of it. He looked at Lucy's house to the left and back to that big ugly apartment building that was going up on the right side of his house. Soon, when he sat out here, the people in that building would be able to look down on him from their windows. They were all three-and four-bedders, twenty-two of them, he'd read on the signs that were creeping their way too close to his front footpath. They'll be families, he imagined, too many of them shoved into too small a space and the noise of this neighbourhood will stretch all the way from Church Street to here, to his space. There'll be no escape.

He finished the first of his son's skinny cigarettes and started another one. Everything slowed down. He looked up at the skeleton of the building next to him, imagined people pouring out of the window frames likes waves of water and bodies everywhere splashing out onto the concrete of his front yard until it was inundated with people swimming around like it was some kind of giant above-ground swimming pool. He laughed, but he was angry, but he laughed some more. He looked to the side of his house where the cans of blue paint and the brushes he'd cleaned in turpentine were standing drying against the fence. He was trying to look there so he could stop laughing and getting angry at the people swimming on his front lawn.

That's when he saw Nico standing there in the corner next to the paint tins shaking his head. Nico looked disappointed, not just about the people swimming in the yard. He looked disappointed about everything. He'd been standing around just out of Antonio's view for weeks now, sobbing in the darkness. He'd been there, standing in the glare of the sun when Fat Frank had told Antonio that he and Nico were too old to be working on building sites anyway. He'd been silent in the doorway when the man from WorkCover had implied that what Nico and he had done that day was irresponsible. He'd been listening when the real estate agent had laughed at Antonio for saying there were too many apartments going up next door. He'd been watching when those kids pushed Antonio over in the street. And now, when Antonio turned to Nico standing there he had nothing to tell him, no way of explaining it all and Nico didn't look like he was willing to listen anyway. Antonio wanted to say *sorry*, but he'd forgotten how to speak. And Nico, still, said nothing, had no wisdom to impart this time. Antonio watched Nico as he leaned over quietly, picked up a paintbrush and held it out towards him.

15.

She'd left teaching because of a hat. Actually, like everything, the story was much more complicated than that, but the simple version was that it all ended with the type of hat that Paul had rocked up to work in today, one of those 59Fifty hats with the wide brims, too big for any real head so that they slipped down slightly over the wearer's eyes. That made it easier, of course, to see the silver sticker that was stuck on the brim, the one all the young guys leave, like displaying a price tag, except this price tag was much cooler because it was shiny and it was a sticker and it told everyone else that you had the money to buy a brand new hat.

Clare watched Paul's hat bob up and down near the counter where he was pulling books out of a box and checking them off on the stock list.

'You going to wear that all day?'

'What?' He looked up, tilted his head back so that he could find some place to see her from behind his fringe and the rim of his hat.

'Your hat. You know. You don't wear hats indoors.'

'Oh. Right. Sorry.' He took it off like an obedient school child and ran his fingers through his hair, placed it behind the counter and got back to unpacking.

Clare stood behind the counter. Watched the street outside.

Again, she felt bad about talking to him like she was his

teacher but she didn't have any real inclination to behave like a better human being, not today, maybe not ever.

She picked up his hat and held it in front of her face like she was about to have a conversation with it.

'Why do you boys always keep the sticker on it?'

Paul leaned up against the counter. He was so thin, like he should still be in Year Ten. He smiled at her, his bottom teeth were all crooked.

'Because it's cool.'

'Why?'

'Because it is.' He smiled at her the way you smile at adults when you're a teenager and you're convinced they don't know anything.

Clare put the hat back on the counter.

'You don't need an explanation for everything.'

She breathed in slowly. Things were quiet today, slow. Paul went back to unpacking books. She watched the two customers in the shop wander the aisles, picking up the books and reading passages from them like it was a library or something.

She wondered if Paul knew the story. Probably he did. *That boy*, she thinks, had been in his year. For a while she felt like everyone she looked at in Parramatta knew the story and so she avoided going home. The wearer of The Hat That Was Her Undoing was a twelve-year-old named Ahmed with so many fat freckles that they had begun to merge across his face so that he looked like he was sporting a patchy tan. He was in her maths class. The one the school made her teach even though she could barely add up. She was trying to show them how long division worked on the blackboard but she wasn't doing it right, there were too many rows of numbers and she'd forgotten to carry one forward and skip a row or a space or something, it made no sense to her. She kept coming up with fifty-four divides into three hundred twelve times but even she knew that wasn't right. She'd turned her back on the class too often and they were throwing bits of paper at each other. Someone's hair got pulled, someone screamed and then when she turned around again Ahmed was still wearing the hat, the one she'd told him to take off about four times already.

'Take . . . off . . . the . . . hat . . . Ahmed,' she'd said slowly and loudly as the whole classroom began to disintegrate. 'Take it off.' It was the only thing she could see herself getting right at that moment. Everything else had gone to shit.

Ahmed had leaned back on his chair balancing on just one chair leg with his foot up under the table precariously keeping him hanging there. He looked up at her and scrunched up his face so that it became hard and sour and said 'No.'

At that moment one of the girls in the back of the class got up and started to cry. The three cool girls sitting near her smacked lip gloss across their mouths and laughed. The crying girl made a run for the door and the pudgy girl no one liked got up and ran after her.

'Get back in your chairs,' Clare had yelled but no one listened, and then Ahmed began to laugh. She lunged forward and grabbed the hat off his head and he fell backwards hitting his head with a thump on the table behind him and then a crack as it hit the floor.

Later, after the ambulance had been called and they'd found three of her missing students smoking in the alleyway behind the school, she was sitting in the principal's office in the naughty chair where he spoke to misbehaving students. He wanted to know why so many students had left her class and why she was letting them lean back on their chairs and why they weren't following her directions. She wanted to say 'long division', but she knew he wouldn't accept that as an answer. She looked out the doorway where the three lip-gloss girls were trying to listen in. What were their names? She couldn't remember.

'I've spoken to some of the kids in your class. They're saying you might have pushed him? I know you've been having a hard time . . . but . . . did you push him, Clare?' She was never, even to this day, sure how he meant it. He seemed fed up, not just with her but because he was tasked with the job of investigating such things. It was obvious this issue had been shoved into a long schedule of meetings, with kids who showed up late to school, and a boy who had thrown an apple at someone else in the playground and the school secretary who was always on the phone to her mother, and Clare was just another nuisance, someone to whom he was obliged to ask a bunch of questions that both bored the shit out of him and made him feel uncomfortable. He straightened himself up again and shoved his hands deeper into his pockets and repeated, 'Did you push him, Clare?'

She had looked at her handbag sitting next to the chair, looked back out into the hallway where the lip-gloss girls were edging closer to the door and smiling mischievously. She picked up her bag, walked out the door, walked through the hallway and out of the school gates, crossed the road to the train station and didn't stop until she was back in Surry Hills. That was it. She didn't return phone calls, never looked back. She still had the letter of termination they sent her underneath her bed.

Two shelves away from where she was standing at the counter, Paul was taking out the travel guides and showing them to a customer. The customer was young, twentyish, with jeans that had holes cut in them. She played with her nose ring while Paul opened up the books and showed her passages.

'Here,' he said. 'This is the nicest place in Vietnam. Đà Lạt. It's in the mountains, it's like the Blue Mountains of Vietnam. It's cooler there, they have really nice gardens and markets and you can cycle all over the place. There's lots of students and universities. It's very French, they even have an Eiffel Tower and you can have French-Vietnamese food there. The French colonised it a long time ago, their houses are still there in the mountains.'

Clare watched the woman take a little notebook out of her purse. She wrote down what he was saying and said, 'Thanks, thanks so much,' before she left without purchasing anything. When she had gone, Paul looked at Clare and smiled.

'It's not a library, Paul. The aim is to get them to buy the books.'

His smile wavered into a nervous frown. 'I was just being helpful. I can't help it if they don't want to buy anything.' He shoved his hands deep into the pockets of his pants and fussed over the display in the front window, straightening up books that were already straight.

'It's just that, that's how we make money you know, selling things. If we don't sell things, we don't have a job, we don't get paid, I can't feed my cat.' She didn't have a cat. She was trying to get herself out of that feeling that she had made someone feel bad again but she was just digging herself in deeper.

She changed the topic. 'So when was the last time you went to Đà Lạt?'

He straightened himself up and looked at her like someone who was ready to fight the schoolyard bully. 'Never.'

'Never?'

'Never. My parents are from there. They told me about it.'

'Oh. Have you ever been to Vietnam?'

'No. My mum came here when she was pregnant with me. They escaped, you know, after the war. My dad was an interpreter with the South Vietnamese army. When the war ended he was put in a re-education camp for a few years, after that they were in a refugee camp in Thailand, then here.'

'Oh right.' She smiled. It made something in the right side of her face itch. She dusted the clean counter with the cloth they kept beside the register. 'You should go there one day.'

'Yeah,' Paul let go of a small laugh. 'Maybe. My parents want to go back but they're always working and there are so many family members needing money. Maybe if I sell some more books I can take them there?'

'Or maybe with the salary you earn when you finish that law degree you're doing?' She curled her hands into tight fists. It wasn't a good joke.

'Or maybe you could go there on all those holidays you teachers get.'

She released her fingers and laughed. 'Yeah, maybe. You know that's all we do, teachers, just have holidays.'

She was glad, now they were both liars, that it allowed for this little secret between them. It was something, some way to connect. In her handbag behind the counter her mobile phone was ringing. It took her a few minutes to realise what was making all the noise. Her father had bought her the phone. She didn't think she needed it but it made him feel safer about her living in Surry Hills. She'd only recently taken to carrying it around, using it occasionally, but it cost a fortune. When she answered, her mother was on the line.

'Quick,' she said, 'call me back on your landline,' and hung up. Her mother thought it was too expensive too.

She waited a few minutes before she called back. Where was she supposed to say she was? It was late in the afternoon. It didn't matter. She wasn't supposed to be at school at this time anyway. She picked up the shop phone and called her mother back at home.

'Where are you?' was the first thing her mother said when she picked up the phone.

'Out, just out in the city. I'm at a pay phone.'

Paul looked at her curiously, walked over to a customer who had just entered the shop and said loudly, 'Can I help you? What books would you like to purchase?' He looked back at Clare and smiled.

On the phone her mother was saying, 'I need you to come home, now.'

'I can't come home right now. I'm busy. How about tomorrow afternoon?' But her mother kept insisting, *now*, she needed to come home *right now*. There was something wrong with her father. The first thing Clare thought was *heart attack.*

'What? Is he sick?'

Her mother kept changing her mind, 'Yes he is sick, but no not like hospital sick. Another kind of sick. You should see what he's painted on the concrete in front of the house.'

Her mother's voice on the phone was distant, sad.

'What exactly is wrong with him?' Clare kept saying, but her mother couldn't explain it.

Then she began to cry, softly down the phone.

Clare didn't know what to do so she said, 'Okay. It's alright. I'll come home. Soon. An hour or so. Can you wait an hour or so?'

There was a pause on the phone. She could hear her mother steady her breathing before she replied. 'Yes, alright, an hour. Just come home. Your father needs you.'

Clare hung up the phone. Looked at her hands. Her mother was usually a calm person. It was her father who was prone to fits and outbursts. She didn't know what was going on but her mother wasn't usually one to make demands. She stood still, tried to think. The shop needed to stay open for another three hours and she was the one in charge of locking it up. She couldn't leave Paul. He didn't know how to count up the till at the end of the day, didn't know how to lock everything down. She picked up the phone again and dialled her manager but she didn't get an answer.

Paul walked triumphantly up to her holding out a copy of *Men Are from Mars, Women Are from Venus* and put it on the counter in front of Clare with a giant grin.

'This lady would like to make a purchase. Here you go. Clare will ring it up for you.'

He stood beside the woman as she pulled twenties from her purse. Clare rung it up twice before the correct number came up on the screen. She took the twenties from the woman's hand. She couldn't find the brown paper bags so she just handed it over.

'Enjoy your book,' she said out of habit as the woman walked out the door.

Paul kept standing there. 'Is something wrong?'

'I need to go. I've got a family emergency. I need you to take over the shop. Can you call Ben? I can't get ahold of him. Tell him you're in charge. I had to go. I have an emergency.'

She took the keys out from behind the counter. 'I can't leave you with these I don't think. Or maybe you could just lock up and take them over to my place later. Or maybe not. I don't know. I need them to open the shop in the morning.'

'It's fine. Clare. It's fine. I can shut up the shop. I've watched you do it a couple of times now. Your family doesn't live that far from mine do they? I can take them there later. Whenever you want. I'm not in tomorrow. But I can take back the keys. No problem. I'll call Ben. No problem. You just take care of whatever you need to do.'

She picked up her purse. Tried to think of more instructions. There were more instructions she should give him, she was sure, but she needed to walk out, just like she did that day at school. She needed to be somewhere else.

'Go. You need to go.'

Right. Good. She picked up her handbag. She needed to go. She walked out of the shop. Paul stood there at the doorway.

'Go,' he said again. 'It'll be fine. I'll bring the keys back to you.'

16

There were too many cars on his street so Francis parked his ute two blocks from home and walked back. The words in the concrete underneath his feet said the same thing every few metres, *Jesus Saves*. He practised not stepping on cracks like he did when he was a child (step on a crack, break your father's back!).

Now he was turning the corner. Now he was looking towards his home from across the street. Now he was noticing that a large piece of the white picket fence had fallen down and was lying on the pavement. Now he was slapped in the face by that giant image in blue paint that took up every inch of the concrete lawn in front of his house. *No More Boats*. It was written in shaky letters in the middle of a circle with a slash through it. On further inspection Francis saw that a little sail boat was drawn in there too underneath the lettering, in case someone didn't get the message.

Sometimes he felt like shit only happened at his place, and as he stood there on the other side of the road where all the houses were quiet and still, he knew it had to be true. Some other things that were beginning to grab his attention: two kids, fifteenish, standing on their skateboards in the gutter throwing pebbles at the windows of his home; an older man in khakis taking photographs of the house with a giant black camera; the builders from the site next door hanging over the fence, pointing and arguing, flicking their cigarette butts over onto the driveway. Also, the noise, nothing distinguishable, just a kind of low buzz around the place like things were about to start happening. SUVs and bashed-up Hondas drove by, slowed down, people stuck their heads out car windows and pointed. An old man from the retirement home down the road was sitting on his white plastic chair at the very corner of its lawn so that he could watch all the action with his arms folded across his lap.

And so, because he couldn't think of a better plan, Francis crossed the road, looking straight at the side of the house like something important was waiting for him there, and just kept going, even when he felt the hard flick of pebbles hitting the back of his head.

Around the side of the house there was a tin of paint knocked over. Its blue insides crept into the bushes next to where a paint brush had been left to dry. He made his way to the back and through the sliding glass doors on the porch. Inside, after all the business of the outside, there was only silence.

In the kitchen: no one; in the living room: no one. In the bedroom his father was lying underneath a sheet, snoring, his bare shoulders poking up over the top. Francis realised he had not been inside his parents' room in years. It was something of a shock to see it now, to realise it looked the same, to be so close to his father lying barely clothed underneath a sheet. There were the pictures of him and Clare as children sitting on the bedside table. There's Clare—always with that look on her face as if she knows everything that's coming—her hair in tight braids on each side of her head, standing at attention, waiting to be praised. Francis stood right next to her, his face knitted together with frustration, maybe because his sister was leaning her hand on his head or maybe because the world had already become so hard to understand and he hadn't yet discovered all the mind-altering substances that would make him think he did get it, even if only for a short moment. Those ugly paintings of flowers his mother bought at a garage sale years ago were still on the wall, the bright yellow of sunflowers, faded now to the colour of mustard vomit.

He went to the window and peered through the venetians. Outside, the kids on skateboards had gone but the cars were now slowing down to a stop. Two Islander-looking women got out of a purple ute and took photographs of each other in front of the house. He looked back at his dad—still sleeping. The man before him was old now, he could see, older than the image he had of him in his head. His father's hair had turned completely white and sat in sparse clumps. He'd gotten old and mad, or maybe he'd always been mad and had just started getting old. That rotted statue of St. Francis had made its way from where it had shown up in the living room and was now sitting on the table beside his bed.

And now? What do I do now? He turned around and walked back into the kitchen where he knew his mother kept her little address book in the drawer. He found the number for the mobile phone his dad gave his sister and did something he never did, he called her up. It was Clare who asked the first question straight after he'd said 'hi'.

'Do you know what your father did?' she asked as if she had no part in the family. That question. It was always coming back at him like someone throwing a rock at his head from behind. Before he could find anything to say he looked up to catch the back of his father as he walked towards the front door, his silent movements aided by the fact that he was wearing no shoes, no clothes, nothing but his underwear. The silence only made the opening of the front door even louder. Francis dropped the phone. He caught up to his father just as half a dozen eggs came flying into the house. When Francis slammed the door shut, it sounded as though another dozen hit the door with a wet thud. His father didn't move. He just stood there with arms folded, staring at the door like he was ready for a fight but didn't know where to find one.

Francis held his father's elbow gently and guided him towards the couch. He didn't resist, he just sat down in that same space where the indent in the cushion said he'd been many times before.

Francis swallowed hard and spoke softly. 'What are you doing, Dad?'

'Me? What are they doing out there? Too many people. So much fuss. All those boats. Too many boats.'

His father looked confused and tired. The white cotton of his underwear was stained with egg yolk and it was threadbare, so that it had become almost see-through, exposing the outline of his flaccid penis beneath. Francis couldn't bear to look at him. From the kitchen he heard his sister shouting through the phone he hadn't put back on the receiver.

17

And so, shortly after her brother hung up on her, Clare's black patent-leather pump emerged from the door of a taxi and placed itself firmly on the bitumen across the road from her childhood home. On the pavement to the right of the house an ancient man sat on a plastic chair with a picture of Pauline Hanson resting against the lower half of his legs. He looked up at her, smiled, as if to say, 'welcome to the show'.

And what a show it was! Two kids in backwards caps stood on the sidewalk, barely trying to hide the eggs that they were carrying in plastic bags behind their backs. Three cops in lycra and fluorescent vests leaned against their bikes and watched the kids, waiting for them to make a move and disrupt the tableau of Socialist Alliance protesters with their not-from-around-here piercings and vintage clothes on pale skin, and the families who had come out to stare, mums, dads, grand-parents, with their I-am-from-around-here pressed saris and knock-off Hermes headscarfs, too much lipstick and Nike shoes.

Clare clutched her purse under her arm. She couldn't quite see the image her mother had tried to describe on the phone. From the apartment building next door two construction workers stood on the unfinished balcony and casually threw cement powder onto the front lawn.

The teenage boys from down the road were making paper airplanes with the Socialist Alliance pamphlets scattered on the ground and flying them into people's hair.

She did not know if she could move forward . . . It was impossible, she thought, to cross over that small expanse of concrete lawn and make it into their house, so she did what her mother did when she was overwhelmed and bypassed the house altogether, stepped onto the front porch of Lucy's house next door and knocked.

In the window to the left of the door she saw Lucy's face and then her mother's, peeking through the blind. It was her mother who opened the door slightly to let her in and then closed it with a sharp thud behind her.

When they were standing in front of each other her mother ran the palms of her hands over her head, like she always did when she was nervous, smoothing down the fuzzy bits of her hair as if it were the fuzziness that was the problem. The sounds of men talking loudly next door crept in through the walls like there was a party they were missing out on at home.

Clare kissed her mother on both cheeks. 'Where's Dad?'

'Home.'

'Alone?'

'With John Solomon.'

'Who's John Solomon?'

'I don't know. Some man. He showed up to help out your dad this afternoon.'

'I'm not so sure that Dad is very helpable anymore.'

Her mum sat down on the little bench Lucy kept in the hallway.

'He's a nuisance, that man.'

That's it. That's all her mother had to say. Her husband was a nuisance, as if he were some kind of child that needed to be tamed. Sometimes all Clare really wanted was for her mother to be furious. At someone, anyone, if only to prove that she was really real and not some woman from a 1950s sitcom. Through the door in the alcove she could see Lucy sitting on the couch, turning on the TV. Clare sat down next to her mother, watched her fold and refold her hands over each other, the same way she had done all her life. Her mother had never been able to recognise her own significance. She wondered sometimes how it was that her mother had ever ended up with her father. She suspected it had something to do with them finding each other exotic; her father and his clichéd Italian swarthiness and her mother the Australian-born daughter of an English Rose. In the distance Clare could hear Lucy flipping through the TV channels; something about Tampa on the news briefly, more boats on another channel, then she stopped at Australia's Funniest Home Videos.

Unlike her mother, Clare had no stamina for silence. After a couple of minutes watching her mother's hands in the hallway she spat out, 'And what now? What happens now?'

On her face her mother wore her 'I'm thinking about it' look a little too long, so Clare stood up as if this would achieve something. Rose looked up at Clare, tears in the corners of her eyes, maybe (or perhaps Clare just wanted them to be there), and said, 'I don't know.' Canned laughter and the darkly comic sound of calamity swept out of the living room and into the hallway where they were sitting.

'That Australia's Funniest Home Videos is really funny,' her mother said flatly. Clare held out her arm to pull her mother up. There was no point in asking sensible questions. She bit the inside of her cheek and tried to shut up because she knew that that was what everyone needed.

'Let's go watch it then.'

Lucy looked up at the two of them as they entered the living room and caught Clare's eye. Clare could see she was dying to give her commentary on the situation. She was glad when Lucy said nothing, just cocked her head slightly, a little gesture from the implicit conversation she and Clare had been having since childhood. The gesture came out whenever she and Clare were agreeing that something her father had done should be met with disapproval. Her mother never joined in on their silent conversation, though Clare suspected she knew what was being said.

When the three of them were tight up against each other on the couch, warming themselves in the TV glow, Clare's phone began to beep in her backside pocket. 'U OK?' the message on the screen said. It took her too long to work out what the letters stood for—obvious words, and that it had to be Paul.

'Yep,' she texted back. Then thought she better clarify— 'Yes I am fine', she texted.

'At home?'

'In Parra.'

'If you give me the address I can put them in your mailbox later tonight I'm going that way.'

She thought about it for a moment and gave him the address of Lucy's house. She knew she was here for a while, wedged between her mother who was looking at the wall towards their house as if she could see through it, and Lucy who was pretending to be engaged in the TV but was really trying to look at Clare's phone.

'Who is it?' Lucy turned to say to her. 'On the phone?'

'Just someone from work. He's going to drop my keys off later into your mailbox.'

She sat up straight and sighed before pronouncing, 'Thought it might be your father begging for forgiveness.'

Clare looked over at her mother but she was still trying to stare her way through the wall.

'Your man can come in, you know, if he wants.'

'No, not today. Not my man either. Just someone I work with.'

How could she possibly ever explain it to Paul?

Lucy raised her eyebrows at her mother's back and declared, 'Who needs a chocolate biscuit?' before leaving the room without waiting for the answer.

Her mother turned and looked at her, gave a weak smile before shifting her gaze towards the television. Clare looked at her mother's profile, trying to find someone in there, pushing her way back through to the present, to what she'd seen in her sometimes when she could be bothered to look: some kind of resistance like in those times her mother had left to stay with Lucy. But even then, she had only moved next door.

'What?' Rose said softly, still not looking her in the eyes.

'Just . . . do something.'

It made Clare want to punch someone, just sitting there. Instead, she picked at the loose threads of her skirt. Inadmissible thoughts.

Clare forced herself now to be someone else, the daughter with the nice personality who was visiting her mother from out of town. She slowed down her breathing, watched the loose threads on her skirt. It was stuffy in here. Almost hot. The weather was preparing to drift into summer. Her mother sank down into the couch and yawned. Lucy came back with a packet of chocolate biscuits, a bottle of cherry brandy and three small glasses. She watched Lucy pour the drinks, the ritual of these two women clinking small glasses together without even considering their action, same as she had all her life. Her mother exhaled cherry brandy breath beside her.

'It's too hot,' Clare said suddenly, surprising even herself as the words she was thinking in her head popped out of her mouth without her permission. On the street outside—the sound of tires screeching, feet running. Someone screamed.

'I'm going to go outside. Get some air.'

Her mother didn't look up. Scoffed her brandy and poured another. Nodded her head. That was it.

Clare stepped cautiously on the porch as though it would help stave off any unwanted attention from people on the street who couldn't care less about her. Somewhere between the lights of windows and street lamps and cars, she could see a twentyish woman in leopard-print pants being consoled by another girl with the same brown ponytail and gold ballet flats.

'It's alright,' she was saying, 'the paint will come out and besides it matches anyways. The paint and the leopard print.'

Mostly, everyone else seemed to be walking off down the road now, in different directions. She looked at the front pavement of her yard and quickly worked out why the show was over. Someone had thrown balloons full of white paint everywhere. They had burst on the fence and the concrete as if the front yard had been shot up with a giant paintball gun. One paint balloon sat like an oversized egg in the middle of the image her father had painted there. The word 'Boats' was largely wiped out in the attack, along with most of the image of a boat. 'No More' sat by itself underneath the top arch of a circle like an omen.

When she looked up someone was waving. Paul. Across the road. He pulled himself off the white van he was leaning against and walked over towards her with a set of keys in his hand.

'I just saw the most incredible thing,' he said. 'These guys in a lowered Honda, they pulled up in front of your neighbour's house and threw paint balloons at this giant picture of a boat in the front. I think it said "no more boats".'

She looked past him to the van. 'What's in the van?'

'Nothing. Rows and rows of racks that we put the bread on in the morning before we deliver it places.'

He placed the keys in her hand and looked over to the house again where her father was creeping out from the left side, a great big plank of wood in his hand.

'Man, you've got some fucked up neighbours there.'

It was too hot outside as well. The heat sat heavily on her skin. 'Take me somewhere,' she said when he was up close, startling him so that he almost fell back.

'Where?'

She looked back at her father who was just behind the side gate now, peering cautiously over, picking up more loose bits of wood and rock, like he was getting ready to launch a one-man assault. For a moment when he looked up he caught her eye, and looked at her blankly until a small balloon flew by the side of his face, distracting him. Clare turned to Paul, 'Take me anywhere.'

He ran his hand back straight through his hair and lifted it off his eyes so that he could really look at her. 'Alright.'

In Paul's van there was some kind of jazz playing. Not what she had expected. Clare would have pegged him for an R'n'B man like her brother—but he had layers, she was beginning to realise. People grow up, or maybe he was always more grown-up than she had given him credit for. At this moment he must have felt like more of an adult than she was.

They headed down Victoria Road towards the city and she wound down the window. Words had deserted her, finally. She did not feel any pressure to speak. Her hair slipped out of the clip she had tied it in, wisps of the blond streaks the hairdresser put in last week moved around her face in the breeze from the open window, distracting her, and suddenly she felt completely sure she had not remembered to button her pants. Everything was surreal. At one point in time, in some younger day, she had always meant to own a van like this with a mattress in the back so that she could drive somewhere, anywhere, out of here. She touched the crotch of her pants lightly. Everything was buttoned. Check. The van smelled of buttery pastry. She wanted to lick the air.

When they stopped it was in a side street underneath the Harbour Bridge. Paul got out and walked towards a small ferry pier there, across the harbour from Luna Park. So close to the city and it was quiet and still. They sat cross-legged on the planks of the ferry pier, only the heavy sounds of the water beneath them. Paul stretched out his legs.

'I like it here. I like just sitting here, watching the boats come in under the bridge. Your neighbour would hate it, I suppose. Not a boat man.'

'That's my dad. The man next door. Except it's my parents' place. You picked me up at the neighbours.'

In the light, his face looked etched. People looked different when they were not moving. A small yacht sailed by, a woman on the bow waved at them sitting there.

'Sometimes I have dreams about it, you know. Coming to Australia on this small overcrowded fishing boat. It's totally like the whole boat-people story you see on the news. I see those incessant waves hitting the boat, people lying in the dark in the ship's hull, clutching children, throwing up all over one another in silence. Actually, my family came on a plane when my mother was pregnant with me. We were one of the last Vietnamese refugee families to come here in the early eighties. But you know, I still imagine we came by boat.'

'My dad, you know, he was a boat person. He came in at the end of the whole populate-or-perish thing in the late '50s. Not as a refugee, but you know, still on those boats he seems to hate at the moment.'

'What's his problem?'

'Don't know, really, probably a lot of things. I just think, he's old and he's angry that he's not in control anymore. He's always had a thing about migrants these days not working as hard, not trying to fit in as much as he did but, you know, it's nothing extreme, just the usual racism, I guess. His best friend died recently and he was forced to retire. That's it maybe, he can't handle change.'

Paul nodded his head, breathed deeply. 'You going back to Surry Hills or Parra tonight?'

She watched the water. Parramatta. She couldn't stand the thought of it. She could either be with her mother who had nothing to say, or her father who had too much.

'Can you take me back to Surry Hills?'

This late at night the trip was quick. She was so tired and not tired at the same time. There were too many things going on in her head and she couldn't make sense of them. She watched Paul flick the van into park and noticed for the first time that he wasn't as frail as she had imagined he was.

His arms were solid-looking, sturdy. The muscle on his upper left arm stood out with the small flex required by the shift in gears. Outside, the weather was changing now; she could feel that cool wet in the air that comes after a sudden snap of heat. It was the kind of wet that brought you out of yourself again.

'Clare? This is it, isn't it? Your place?' She looked at him again. Realised that they must have passed too much time in silence since they pulled up there, while she was looking at his arm.

'Yes,' she leant over and picked up her purse. There was a scar just underneath his chin. She couldn't read him, couldn't tell what he was thinking, he tapped his hands against the steering wheel and watched her like he was really trying hard to understand something about her. Maybe he was someone completely different to what she had imagined. Outside it was beginning to rain. The wet was creeping its way into her skin and she was starting to feel more awake than she had felt in a long time. She leant closer to him and said, 'I think you should come upstairs.'

18.

The morning after. Rose stood on Lucy's front porch in an old red silk slip that Lucy had lent her to sleep in, and the felt overcoat she was wearing when she came over the previous night. In her hand there was a mug of tea, strong to make the hangover fade quickly. This morning she was the only person in the universe. The cars were gone, Lucy was asleep, the street had stilled itself. Her daughter left with a man last night without even saying goodbye.

Clare didn't think Rose knew what she got up to, but she had seen it, the desire. She knew Antonio had seen it too. Rose watched them both from the window of Lucy's house last night: Clare getting into a van with a young Asian man, Antonio, plank in hand, standing at the side of their house watching Clare.

Her daughter had had lots of men, or men had had lots of her. Rose was not sure, but she had watched these boys come and go over the years. Clare never seemed to like anyone enough to want them to stick around. What Clare did not understand was that you had to give a bit, and you had to stay a bit, and sometimes you just needed to be quiet for a while.

And sometimes you needed to get away from someone for a while if you were going to stay with them. Rose had done that too, done it more than Clare realised. That was, after all, why there was such a large age gap between her children, because she had moved next door with Lucy for a couple of years in between having Clare and Francis. Clare hadn't seemed to notice. She had just waved at her absent father over the fence and gone back inside the house to play with Lucy and Stone.

Lucy and Stone. She had not thought of Stone in a very long time. What was her real name? Something like Samantha. It was the early 1970s and everyone had to be someone slightly different from themselves to make a point about something. Stone made Rose realise that she could fill an ocean with the things she did not know, like for example that women could be lovers, or that they were fighting wars over in Vietnam with chemicals that made your skin melt off your bones.

If you turned on the television back then, everyone was moving and shaking, everyone knew a lot of things and had a lot to say about it. Rose and Lucy knew so much about how to make cheap meat off-cuts into a giant shepherd's pie, and which industrial cleaners didn't make your skin itch so much, and how to rub lavender into the sweaty spots on your arms and legs so that you didn't smell like you'd been working in the kitchen of a hostel all day when you went for a dance at the Polish Club after work.

Lucy had met Stone in those first couple of years when Rose was absent. She had not been absent in any real sense; it was just that after Clare was born, she had trouble being completely present. It was like, one moment she could be there sipping a cup of tea, rocking Clare's bassinet, and everything was sharp-edged and bright, and then she was in a fog again and it was as though she was speaking through plastic.

Rose looked over to her own front yard where Antonio had emerged. His thick cargo work pants rolled neatly up past his ankles, his black boots on. In his right hand he was carrying a bucket with several objects inside. Above him, two of the construction workers looked down from the balcony of the apartment block and watched him. Antonio obviously saw nothing but the concrete on the ground before him. She watched him put his cane down on the ground gently, watched him lean over and support his descent to the ground with his good arm. He pulled a sponge from his bucket and started to scrub the ground.

For a moment she saw Antonio as those two construction workers would have seen him. His skin had that leathery tan of old age, still with muscles protruding from beneath his saggy skin. His white hair was unclipped, wild, but there was something in the efficiency of the way he moved that said this man meant business—he had a plan.

She would talk to him about all this business when the time was right—Antonio, her lost lover, her husband, was disappearing into something, she did not know what. She pulled the belt of her overcoat tightly in around her waist and stepped into Lucy's yard barefooted. As she crossed over from Lucy's yard to her own she knew that she was entering something, the beginning or the ending of a chapter in their lives, she did not know which.

She watched him for a while, from the other side of their front gate, until he looked up and smiled at her and she got caught there not knowing how to respond. Yesterday morning she had asked him calmly, rationally, to remove the paint from their front yard and just when she'd almost returned him from some irrational argument about Nico turning up in their front yard, this guy John Solomon had showed up at their door from some kind of political organisation, saying that Antonio was a hero. He'd shaken Antonio's hand firmly, gripped his shoulder and squeezed it in camaraderie, as if he was a lieutenant welcoming back his most prized soldier. Then the logical world she had tried to pull Antonio back into began to fall apart again.

But now. Here was her home. Here was her husband smiling at her. Here was Antonio doing exactly what she asked him to do, cleaning a mistake off the concrete. So she smiled back, walked closer to him, put her hand against his shoulder as he leaned over.

'Hey.'

'Hi,' he said, leaning back to sit on the ground like a child. She considered leaning over to pull him up into her arms but didn't.

'How about I make us some coffee, some breakfast too? I've got some eggs in the fridge. You could come in when you're done. We could just eat, relax. Today, we don't need to do anything.'

'Right. Great. Eggs. I've got to finish this and then I've got some work to do this afternoon but good. We should sit, have breakfast.'

'Okay,' Rose touched him lightly on the shoulder again and entered her house. It was dark inside and the house had the presence of other people there, a jacket she didn't recognise was hanging over the arm of a chair. Folders and binders and books that didn't belong in her house were stacked in neat piles on the dining-room table.

She would not spend time thinking about these things today. She wanted to make coffee and eggs and take a shower and maybe watch an afternoon movie on the television with Antonio.

She put the kettle on to boil, got the container of eggs out of the fridge. There was a kind of weight to being here that made her feel tied down. She thought for a moment of returning to Lucy's, but instead, she leaned against the countertop and looked out of the kitchen towards the garden where things, as always, needed some help. Being in someone else's house required less of you. Being in your own home, you had to be yourself and that was harder. It's the house really. A house gave you a shape to fit your life into. The house had turned her into the kind of woman who tried to care about fingerprints on windows and dirty dishes in the sink. The kind of woman who wondered whether or not her children were happy when she heard the way they dragged their feet across a carpeted floor.

Sometimes she imagined what might have happened if she had stayed next door, if she would have turned into a woman, like Lucy, who tiled her own bathroom and took a woman for a lover, who did courses in night school when Whitlam made it free and drank cherry brandy sitting in gumboots on her front verandah most nights and who didn't care if anyone noticed.

In the kitchen she felt the presence of the other woman she could have been. The kettle boiled. She spooned instant coffee and sugar into two cups. Maybe she could have gone to university like her daughter and had lots of different choices about what she could do with her life. Maybe she could have run her own business or backpacked around the world, she could have been someone that people took more notice of.

That day, a week before she moved out of Surry Hills as a sixteen-year-old to Villawood with all her possessions in one small suitcase, she'd been the one to find her mother hanging by a sheet fixed to an exposed roof beam in the basement laundry of that old terrace house. Her mother had always wanted so much more than a house full of boarders. She'd wanted trips to the theatre and Sunday afternoon roasts with her family who lived on another continent. She'd wanted someone to take care of her. She'd wanted a rest.

What Rose wanted to tell her children was that she had worked so hard for so long, that it was hard to be present and happy and graceful and kind. It was hard to be faithful and good. All you can do is to try to inhabit a life, to love it because it's yours. Neither of her children had ever put in that kind of effort, had ever committed to the self-sacrifice and discipline that it took to try to be happy in your own skin.

19

Harold Holt was eaten by a shark because he relaxed the White Australia Policy. The bloke with the shaved head sitting across from Antonio at a busted-up kitchen table in an old terrace in Tempe was explaining this to the others. He liked the idea of the sea reaching up in violent retribution and tearing Harold Holt to bits for beginning the country's downfall.

It was Thursday, and although Antonio had been excited about coming here before, now he was not so sure. There was something about the place that unsettled him. The floors that looked like they were not vacuumed enough. The bust of Ned Kelly that had clearly never been dusted, the Eureka flag that had the faded shapes of rectangles permanently impressed on it from the light that shone in between the gaps in the thick bars on the windows.

The whole place had the look and feel of a cubby house for teenage boys. There were the two pasty-looking young men with shaved heads and bulky lace-up boots like boys playing at being in the army. There were three other men, more respectable-looking in chinos and collared shirts, and a woman who looked like the girlfriend of a bikie—she just nodded her head in agreement with everything and tapped her plastic orange nails on the table. But there was also John. John Solomon, who had appeared in front of Antonio's house dressed in a black suit with a megaphone hanging off his arm. John Solomon who had quoted Arthur Calwell, William Lane and John Curtin in his firm and demanding voice to all the people gathered there. Antonio wasn't quite sure who those people were, but from the gist of what John Solomon said they were great Australians and he thought Antonio was a great Australian too.

John Solomon kept on talking and Antonio went back inside himself even though it was a hard thing to do with him standing there, John Solomon just had this kind of voice, this way of standing so unwaveringly straight that meant you couldn't help but pay attention to him. Antonio just didn't know what he was doing here, or at home, or anywhere really. Nico had told him to paint that sign on the front lawn and then John Solomon had told him to keep it there. John Solomon reminded him of the Nico he'd known twenty years ago, built big and broad like a labourer in his prime, someone who people said yes to without really knowing why. Rose had moved next door, like she did all that time ago when she'd left him for a few years. He had grown anxious and tired and then he had scrubbed the concrete clean of everything he'd wanted to say. He was lonely but he also wanted to be alone. When he saw all those people on his front lawn, in his space, all he could do was take one of those pills the doctor had given him with a whisky and go back to bed until he woke up at some unidentifiable time of the night or the day and it was still too noisy but at least, at least there was John Solomon and he was helping him make some sense of everything.

And because of all this Antonio was wearing his blue suit. The one he wore when he wanted people to take him seriously.

And because he wanted to show that he was a serious man he had armoured himself against the feeling that no one really took him seriously with a double-breasted jacket and pants that had a sharp crease down the middle.

John Solomon was also wearing a suit. He always wore one. He had a serious face, never smiled, spoke slowly, articulated every word, hung carefully off the vowel sounds so that when he said 'elite lefties' it came out sounding like '*ah*-leat lefties.' He had a plump tanned-white earnest face to match his white hair and he had the body of a giant rectangular box. He was vain of his voice, had been a debating champion and a too-smart-for-his-own-good public nuisance who had grown up in a small town in the far west of the state. His family were some sort of small-business owners. What business they were in John didn't specify to Antonio, but he was fond of saying they were hard-working, ordinary people. He was in fact more aligned to those grubby, leftist anarchists than they would like to think. He was fond of saying nationalism, true nationalism, had its roots in the union movement, in the working classes, in socialist democracy. Antonio was getting to know a lot about John. Yes. John Solomon liked to talk and he liked the sound of his own voice a little too much for Antonio's liking, but he knew a lot of things and there was stuff going on here that Antonio wanted to understand.

When some young thug in a black anarchist shirt had tried to climb through Antonio's window, John Solomon had pulled him out by the legs, just like that, like this young guy was nothing. He just slapped him to the floor and started lecturing him about public property and decency and respect. When he invited Antonio to this 'meeting of like minds', as he called it, what could Antonio say? He owed the man that much and besides, what else was there for him to do these days?

At John Solomon's kitchen table they were having a meeting and the subject of this meeting was Antonio. The meeting began the same way that everything began with John Solomon. He talked about bees. More specifically, the Chinese and their bee-like properties as identified by Australia's most prominent early unionist William Lane. 'Nations,' John Solomon explained, 'have swarming populations like beehives. When nations reach a critical stage of over-population people mass-migrate. Lane said China had a swarming population of sixty-five million and that was the late 1880s. Imagine, now it would be the same for the Middle East. It's happening every moment. We're seeing the effect of those swarming populations sitting in a boat called Tampa, right off our own shores. They're waiting, just waiting to swarm on in and start another hive.' He paused for dramatic effect, pointed his index finger out and waved it around in a slow alarming spiral, before standing, placing his arms behind his back and pacing across the room.

The skinheads shifted restlessly in their chairs. Antonio imagined bees. One of the men in collared top and chinos (what was his name?) suggested that these swarming populations would probably get together with the Aboriginals, because they hate us too, and form some kind of militia and take over.

John Solomon nodded his head gravely, 'We are a vulnerable, underpopulated island, ready for the taking.' Everyone nodded their heads except Antonio, who was still thinking about it: Chinese bees, Aboriginal bees.

'What do you think?' John Solomon looked at Antonio and raised an eyebrow. 'Are we offending you?'

'No. Not offence,' he said suddenly. Such a quick movement out of his thoughts brought out the Italian accent he had managed to suppress most of the time. 'I guess mostly I am concerned that there are too many people.'

'Too many people!' John Solomon picked up his line before Antonio had a chance to finish it and threw it out to the room. The barred windows shook in a constant low murmur as cars zoomed en masse down the Princes Highway outside.

Antonio continued, 'In Parramatta they are building everywhere, next door to my house, you should see there is this gigantic apartment building going up. Meriton. Made of shit. Everyone who lives there will be looking down at me all the time. They'll be looking through my windows into my home. All those people.'

The same man in the collared shirt piped up again. 'There has to be a limit. We can't take everyone.'

'That's the problem,' the woman said. 'They already have taken everyone, 'specially places like Parramatta. They took *everyone.*'

The skinheads shook their heads like they couldn't be more disgusted if they tried. One opened a large packet of Smith's Crisps and poured it into the plastic wood-coloured bowl on the table. The sound of his crunching filled the small room until John Solomon spoke again.

'Exactly! Too many people. And when you tried to stand up to that you were bullied.' He took a deep breath, looked at Antonio. 'Your house was paint-bombed, the anti-democratic left showed up on your lawn and tried to shut down your voice.' John Solomon sat down again then rose up for dramatic effect. 'Now, *nooow,*' like he was the king of everything. 'What are we going to do about it?'

In the next few days, Antonio would lie awake thinking. He'd toss and turn and then leave the house at two or so in the morning because he'd feel as though he might stop breathing if he didn't get out from between those walls. There was this something inside of him, this small pellet of disquiet growing bigger every day. Sometimes when he slept he was sure that he was being watched. When he woke up in the middle of the night he felt as though his sleeping-self had been locked in deep conversation with whomever was in the room and just at that moment, when the discussion had reached the point at which he was about to figure something out, he woke up before he could get any answers and he couldn't remember what questions he was asking anyway. He was missing some essential information somehow, but the knowledge was there right in the back of his brain. One thing he knew for certain was that it was all connected with water. He lay awake thinking of waves, floods, tsunamis. He imagined people, slick like eels, being carried up on the white froth of turbulent water. He imagined them crashing down around him. He thought too of that boat sitting off the shore with its 438 people, just waiting there. Waiting for the moment when they could invade.

20

Francis scooped up the mortar with his trowel, spread it in a slow even line across the top of a row of bricks and then ran the trowel's tip across the mortar to spread it to the edges. He placed the brick down, tapped its top with the trowel's handle and scraped off the excess mortar that oozed out underneath. He buttered the end of the next brick, placed it down, tapping its top with the trowel's handle, scraped off the excess mortar . . . He began again. He liked this aspect of his job, the way you became a machine. After a while he entered into a trance state, like at those nightclubs when he was tripping and it didn't matter if the song kept changing, because he'd already picked up a beat and it'd already got itself inside his bloodstream, and his arms and legs were moving and doing their thing independently of him and he knew that he was alive and he knew that he was a machine at the same time, and the beat and the beat and the beat and he was something holy.

It was, of course, that motherfucker Charbel who drew him out of that Zen space and back into the reality of the rhythmless world he didn't want to be in. In this world the other men on the construction site kept saying things in unusually quiet voices, turning away when he stared. He did hear it though, that one guy, the one who always wore a skull cap, when he walked by him near the cement turner and Francis distinctly heard him say, 'You Australians and your safe, safe lives.'

Safe. Safe. The word had interrupted his thoughts too many times already this morning. He didn't know what the guy meant. And now Charbel was saying 'C'mon, c'mon. Lunch. Don't you think it's time for a little break?' And he realised that he'd been at it since seven and it was twelve now and he needed to pee so badly he was about to urinate out his eyeballs.

Charbel was standing there, cracking his knuckles, same as he had been since they were twelve. As usual he did not look like he'd been doing any of the hard stuff. Here, in this place, the lack of cement flecks on your shirt and mud stains on your pants made you stand out like a homeless guy in a bank. Two men walked behind Charbel, but when Francis caught their eyes they looked away and dropped their voices to a low hum.

'Working hard today?' Francis asked him, pointing to his clean shiny black loafers, but they both knew that Charbel was the one who took his job seriously and the clean pants were all part of that.

They used to work well together when Francis first came to work for Charbel's dad a couple of years back; it was always a kind of competition. Francis could lay down walls much quicker than Charbel but he would always fuck them up some-how—a loose brick, a slight tilt. There was never anything really tense though, not like now when there was a thin layer of bad between them that never got talked about.

Anyway, Francis was still glad, really, for the company of an old friend and his pressed polo shirts. You didn't need to explain yourself to people you'd known for such a long time. You didn't have to talk.

But today Charbel had found something interesting and he'd already got the whole afternoon planned out for them.

'They're at it again,' he said, and Francis wondered if this had something to do with him and all the men on the building site who didn't look at him anymore, until Charbel unrolled the large poster he was holding in his hand.

'They're at it again,' he repeated, 'those Hills Hoist lovers.' He unrolled the poster and held it up for Francis to see.

We believe that all human beings carry with them the potential to live harmoniously together without imposed authority. We regard planners and politicians as dangerous animals—or worse, mechanised robots bent on destruction and personal power. We believe that sufficient wealth and technological know-how exists in the world today to provide a happy life for all people and that does not require them to live one metre apart, in homes that all look the same colour with backyards that cannot accommodate a Hills Hoist.

'Fuckers,' Francis said. 'Where did they leave them now?'

'I don't know. This is the second one I've found around the place. They put padlocks on the gate too. We had to cut them off this morning and they'd painted a wall of one of the display homes green. I keep finding things. Dad thinks we need extra security but I don't think they'll harm anything. They're just hippies and shit who want to paint everything in rainbows so they can be different. How about we get some lunch, have a walk around together, see if they've planted flowers inside one of the portaloos.'

Charbel had their route planned out, start from the perimeters of the estate and then move inward. The largest road on the estate was a giant circle, and inside that was a slightly smaller circular road, and inside that an even smaller one, and in the very middle, a lake. It was near these outside houses that the protesters hung their signs and screwed things up. Once already this year they had broken in and ruined the floorboards of a house by installing an old Hills Hoist right in the middle of the lounge room.

He couldn't understand the protesters (everyone had to live somewhere right?). But still there was something about them that he admired. All that effort to fuck things up, to *creatively* fuck things up. He'd only ever thrown rocks through windows. These guys had some *originality* to the way they destroyed things. He could imagine them after they'd drilled that Hills Hoist in, leaning back against a wall, smoking a joint and laughing to themselves. He wondered if they'd known this place before it was like this. Francis had, though he didn't think about it very much. He used to come here as a child with his dad to visit some family friends who'd lived on a farm. It used to be all fibro shacks in the middle of paddocks. A lot of nothingness interrupted by the odd gum tree. This was the place where he had learned that you can't really tip over cows—not for lack of trying on his part, mind you, but you just can't push them over, even when they're sleeping. They're like concrete blocks on legs— immovable.

Now those cows were all gone. Instead they've got Australian Traditional, Federation, Colonial, American Colonial, Tuscan, Georgian. People like new stuff that looks heritage. One step forward. One step into the past. 'There is no period in history that is finished,' his dad had said.

Before they got going Francis stopped for a piss and Charbel bought them sausage rolls from the lunch truck. They ate on the ledge of a half-built wall. It was, Francis realised, the first time they'd hung out together in a long time, just the two of them. Mostly, they also had Jesús with them, or some other guys from school. On the site and after work they ate lunch or drank beers with their younger workmates, or they'd hang around the demountables playing darts.

Their conversation began on the subject of women. It was the way they got into really talking; it was their version of dis- cussing the weather. Mostly, to be more precise, they talked about their lack of women. It was this complaint that always bound them together, the thing that made them closer to each other than to Jesús 'always-getting-laid' Consalvo. Didn't mat- ter if your dad owned a construction company or your dad painted giant boats in front of your house, it was still hard to get noticed.

When they began their walk, Charbel was talking about Anita, from their school days.

'She's got like two children now and you know most women go to shit after that but I swear, she's looking even better,' he said.

'Man,' Francis cut his eyes towards Charbel. 'Don't you think it's about time you got over that? I mean she's married now, bro. Married.'

'I'd still do her,' he said defensively.

'But what would *that* do?'

'It doesn't have to *do* anything.'

At twenty-three, Charbel still had a dorky teenage quality to him, like he was dressing up in his father's pants because he needed to convince everyone that he was already an adult. But even so he was still doing better than Francis. Already this year he'd had two girlfriends, for a short time, but still, that's something, and yet the moody bastard kept returning to a girl who hadn't acknowledged his existence since way back when they were at school. Francis didn't want to start any arguments so he let it go, just before they made their first discovery on the back wall of one of the completed houses that had sold only last weekend.

There were six stars, each about two feet square, painted in an orange so bright it hurt the eyes, and there was a moon in an iridescent silver. They hung there against the Heritage Blue of the house, a tiny solar system orbiting spilled paint tins on a golf-course perfect strip of lawn.

Charbel lifted his hands up, ran them through his fuzzy black hair and, in an uncharacteristic move, sat on the ground without caring if it'd fuck up his pressed pants. Francis sat down next to him and pulled out a packet of cigarettes. They smoked and stared so hard that the orange was still there when Francis blinked and looked away from the wall to Charbel, whose face appeared to him as though it had taken on an orange glow. Francis watched him take long drags of his cigarette.

Charbel had never been one to think quickly and Francis knew that he thought hard, considered each move.

'It's not that bad,' Francis said. 'I mean, not what they did. The paint job. They can paint and the paint's good paint too. Must have cost them a shitload. All that silver metallic and the neon colours.'

'Waste of paint. Waste of time,' Charbel said, but Francis could tell he was thinking the same by the way he got up close and inspected it.

'I don't know. It's a batshit crazy thing to do but it is kind of good looking, all those stars on blue.'

Charbel looked at Francis like he was mental and gave a half-smile. 'You know my dad has this theory that it's your dad who's done it.'

'That is also batshit crazy.'

Charbel flicked his cigarette to the floor and crushed it underneath his foot. Francis thought; there it is again, that thin bad line. He wasn't sure if this was a stab at him or his father or maybe neither. He knew that now they'd got their talk of women out of the way and were finally alone together, stuff would start to come out.

Charbel said, 'Could be.'

Francis said, 'Could not.'

Then there was a kind of wannabe adult showdown where they sat on the ground next to the painting, under the light of the moon and the stars, so to speak, and they just looked at each other.

He wanted to tell Charbel about something that had happened yesterday: on his mother's request, he had followed his dad to a place in Tempe where he'd watched him enter a terrace with Eureka flags and busts of Ned Kelly behind the iron bars of its windows. He wasn't sure what his father was up to. He felt like any minute something else was going to happen, something worse than boats painted on lawns and stars painted on walls. He watched him walk into that terrace in his blue suit, the one he always wore when he needed people to take him really seriously—his 'I need a loan', 'I need a job' suit, and he wondered what his father needed from these people. Neon orange stars just wasn't what he was up to. He'd gotten himself into something darker than that.

All these things were on the tip of his tongue but he didn't know how to say it to Charbel. Charbel was looking at the stars, cracking his knuckles like he was irritated, like he meant business and he was about to go and sort things out.

'Well whoever it is, I'm not putting up with it.'

He gave Francis a look that said his words were a warning to him, his father and the rest of the world. Francis shrugged his shoulders and lit another cigarette and Charbel went on, 'I'm going to drag that dipshit out of that security booth and show him exactly what is happening while he's watching TV.'

'Yeah,' Francis said, nodding with a kind of enthusiasm he wasn't feeling right now. He just wanted to get back to his bricks and his beats and to being a machine again so he wouldn't have to spend any more time this afternoon trying to figure out how humans work.

'I'll get back to it then.'

Francis walked off in one direction and Charbel the other. When Charbel was out of sight Francis slowed down. He looked at the houses he was passing more closely and tried to remember which walls he had built. He stopped in front of one newly occupied house where all the windows were open, the curtains drawn back. Through the bay windows he could see right into the living room where there was a small kitchen table with four chairs in a huge room full of nothing else. This was one of those things that had always amazed him, the big emptiness of these houses. He thought of those stars, a whole galaxy there like an arrow, drawing attention to that big loneliness.

21

Paul still looked like he belonged in a high school classroom. Those big eyes with too much hair in front of them. For that one moment when he'd come into Clare's house and she'd sat on the couch too close to him and his hand had become wedged between the couch fabric and her thigh for a second too long, she'd thought about inviting him into her bed but didn't.

Mostly, they'd just sat in her living room, drinking and talking and even that had felt like something illicit. He was six years younger, a former student. Now they were both older, the age difference didn't mean so much, perhaps. But still in public, even at the shop, she felt funny to a certain extent talking to him. In her living room no one could see them. When she was alone with him she realised that they were more alike than different. They both had this public side they'd learned to put on and they were both more socially awkward than that façade suggested. They were both from the suburbs. They both had families they wanted to run away from. At first they had those kinds of conversation that Clare was an expert in, where you talked about everything and nothing at the same time, and you only let a little bit of yourself out and, maybe, if you started to feel comfortable, you let out a little more.

And then, their in-the-shop relationship and their out-of-the-shop relationship started to look more alike than different. The two worlds had started to slide up against each other so that the line between being together in public and being together in private was becoming more blurry all the time. Take today, for instance: the bookshop on this September morning. Those customers came in with the fifteen minutes they had before work or the dentist or meeting their lover in a coffee shop down the road, and they wandered the aisles aimlessly, plucking a book from the shelf, putting it back in the wrong place. They came in carrying the smell of hairspray and cheap perfume and croissants, and the breeze they let in through the door ripped open the stuffy air. Clare stood next to Paul behind the counter and read from the letters to the editor section he'd brought from home. This was Paul's weekly gift to her. Mostly, they were all about her father. He'd drawn an ironic love heart in pink around this week's favourite:

No Racist
I am not a racist. My dentist is Chinese and our favourite local butcher is from Korea. I even have an Indian obstetrician—all lovely people! But you know I understand that man with the No More Boats sign on his lawn. We can't let everyone in. Look what's happening with all those Muslim boys harassing white girls because they've got no respect for women.
Signed,
Anonymous Aussie (for fear of persecution in my own country)

It was a strange kind of comfort that the people writing letters in support of her father made even less sense to her than he did. An older man with a gardening manual came to the counter and Clare folded the piece of newspaper up and put it in her back pocket. While she put through the sale Paul was writing his own letter to the editor on the back of one of the brown paper bags they wrapped books in. He pushed it over towards her side of the counter when he was done. It read:

Everyone Came on a Boat
I'm not racist. I'm Vietnamese. I just don't like anyone else. Also, the guy with the No More Boats sign's an ethnic too. He came here on a boat, just like everyone else.

'You going to send it in?'
'Maybe. Got to work on it a bit. You know, finesse it up. Why don't you give me some feedback on it as my former English teacher.'
'Don't do that anymore. Couldn't cope, as you said.'
Paul looked at her and stopped smiling. 'You hanging onto that still? You told me it was true yourself, that you couldn't cope with the teaching. You even said you always hoped a car would hit you on the way to work so you didn't need to go.'
'I'm not hanging on to it.'
'You are.'
She looked away from him because they both knew she was. Her brother and her mum and now Paul, everyone was looking at her life with more insight than she ever had. Things went silent.
They were still testing out where that invisible line lay between them. She was trying too hard not to have a close relationship with him even though she knew she wanted it. Paul kept jumping over the line.
She watched Paul type *paint+bulk+white* into the search engine of the front counter's computer. 'I've got an idea,' he said to Clare in that softly-softly voice men use when they are trying to make amends. 'Maybe there is a simple way that I can help you fix all these issues with your dad.'

22

Antonio was driving down Woodville Road when John Howard told him exactly what he had always known to be true but had never quite put into words before. John Howard said: 'The success or failure of a nation essentially begins in the homes of its people.'

Antonio nodded and said, 'Yes. Exactly!' and kept on driving and listening to the rest of the things that the Prime Minister had to tell him: 'Each one of us is responsible for building our lives and the life of the nation. All of us are accountable to ourselves, to those around us, to the future itself.' And then the Prime Minister was interrupted by an advertisement for mortgage brokers and Antonio turned the radio off because it was those mortgage brokers, on top of everything else, that were currently causing him so much stress that he felt the need to drive and drive.

He was going back to the beginning. To the cul-de-sacs and hexagons and loops that were going to save the world. It'd been his first job in Australia and he'd liked being part of the idealised geometric dreaming of those architects who said that all you had to do to create the perfect community was to give it the perfect shape. No grids! It was called the Radburn Design. It had been explained to him when he walked over from the hostel that first morning; you build a whole community on a hexagon instead of a grid, you turn the houses the other way around so that they face each other and not the street. You have cul-de-sacs everywhere, small alleyways that lead into communal parks; you force people to look at each other and not the road. You make them be a community whether they want to be one or not.

A completely true fact he always remembered: Walt Disney designed Disney World on the same Radburn model because he wanted to inspire people to create better, more cohesive communities. Villawood and Disney World have the same street plan. Imagine that! On the other side of the world there was Minnie Mouse in Tomorrowland, singing songs about friendship and the future in the exact same position on a map as the Villawood Tavern and the Centrelink office.

That last time he'd been out on the housing estate in Macquarie Fields, he'd been trying to tell a young couple he'd met about the Radburns. Matilda and Joe, he liked both of them. He'd shown Matilda how to make the stars she was painting on a wall a little more even-looking by using a spirit level and an old piece of plywood. Antonio had been smoking a joint with Joe and talking about the California Bungalow Joe and Matilda were building out near Richmond-way when suddenly he looked up and there was night-time, rendered more perfectly on that wall than in the sky above him. He'd run into those two a couple of times now, and he always looked for them. Last time, Joe had shown him pictures on his phone of the drainage system he'd built on his property, following Antonio's advice.

And now, as he pulled up in front of that Radburn estate he'd helped to build in Villawood all those years ago, he had all these things in his head. He parked in front of the house he'd bought three years earlier when the Housing Commission had started selling off some of the estate and tearing down the rest of it. Luckily, when it was set on fire there wasn't much structural damage, but the tenants had to be moved out for a while so he wasn't getting any money for rent and then there was the problem of the tenants not wanting to move back in, and of no one else wanting to live there either. Despite all his efforts, and even this late in the night, you could still see the black burn-marks on the bottom edges of the house.

He looked at the house again and thought that at least he could take some comfort in having bought a good house, and in making it the best on this street. He'd built a porch all the way around the front and put in ornate white wooden pillars so that an ordinary old brick box was turned into an Australian Colonial. The builders who had come in to tear down most of the other houses laughed at all the time he'd put into it, but they were too busy building houses that faced the road and whacking those loops of roads into straight grid lines to really listen to anything Antonio had to say.

Now in that same house he could see the dark shadow of a body moving from room to room until all the lights were turned out. He believed in all that stuff the architects said about utopias of hexagons. He still had the article he clipped out of the newspaper a few years ago before they tore half of the houses from the old Radburn design down and sold the rest of it off. 'Everything that could go wrong in a society went wrong,' one of those original planners had said. Who could have realised that if you turned everything into hexagons and loops, then you created all these dark alleyways that let people break in unnoticed? In those discreet little cul-de-sacs and loops, people did whatever they wanted, without anyone being able to see, and eventually the police left them alone, preferring to cruise the safety of the main street where people's lives could be observed more clearly.

When the front of his house had been set on fire, only the others living in that cul-de-sac could see it, and none of those neighbours said anything. That's just the kind of place it was, everyone's house looking at each other, and no one thought they were a part of the rest of the world and its rules.

Antonio got out of his car and stood on the corner. The

road was straight for blocks and blocks until it turned out onto the highway. He'd had his first job here, him and Nico laying concrete and bricks. He'd walked into this space as an olive farmer, and walked out as a man who knew something about building a house. Back then Antonio had never considered that he'd still be trying to prove himself. He'd thought that by this time of his life he wouldn't need to explain to others what he was doing in the world. When you come from nothing, you either accept that you are nothing or you spend the rest of your life trying to be something, until one day you turn around and you realise you might never make it.

23

On the lawn in front of her house, that boat was there again, painted this time in much more purposeful precise strokes. The lettering of 'No More Boats' looked as if it had been done using a stencil. She had gone to the movies with Lucy, and everything had been fine, and then when she returned it wasn't.

This time, when she entered the house he was walking down the hallway towards where she was standing at the front door. She looked at him. He looked at her. He appeared to be standing a little straighter, he was walking without his cane, and even though there was a noticeable limp when he walked, he looked stronger.

Rose pushed her shoulders back in response and stomped her foot down because she could and he couldn't. 'Clean it off,' she said. And then, 'Clean it off now.'

It was, perhaps, the first thing she had ever demanded of him, and she got stuck on repeat, saying it more than a few times just because she couldn't believe that she had said it at all.

'No.' He said it calmly, like he had been waiting all this time for her to object and had already decided that anything she might say was absolutely wrong anyway.

'But why? Why cause so much trouble? So much nonsense. Why? What's the point?'

'Because it is important.'

'Why?'

'To stand up for yourself. It is important. To stand . . . it is important.' And as if to emphasise the point he just stood there. Arms folded, staring at her.

'But why? This isn't the way to stand up for yourself. This is nothing. It's juvenile.'

It made Rose feel dizzy to be talking to Antonio like this— like being at a great height without a rail to hold you back. She had always been the quieter one, the first to back off and give his voice space. She adored him too much, and he spent too much time protecting her. Now, rather late in the game, when they had things to discuss, they didn't possess the kind of language that would allow them to sit down and talk to each other with the ease of two human beings on the same level.

'You know what I mean,' Rose said.

He looked away angry, distracted. His focus was on the cracked paint in the corner of their ceiling. There, right there before her, angrily avoiding her eyes, was the man she'd met at eighteen and thought she knew better than she knew herself. Here he was in the guise of someone who was angry and afraid and confused; she looked at him now and thought he had a kind of ravaged quality she had never seen in him before.

'You don't know anything about it,' he said at length. 'You don't know anything.'

That's when the silence set in, a silence so deep that it took over what had always been a house full of noise. The absence of sound became something so heavy in the air that you could almost touch it, feel it. The silence was everywhere creeping into the curtains, weighing down the couch cushions, withering the leaves of the zucchini plants in the backyard.

Under the weight of all that silence Rose turned and left.

More and more her present was becoming similar to her past, and not like the future she had imagined. Here she was living with Lucy again in a strange, older version of her younger self. Her adult life, her relationship with her husband, a picture of a boat in the front yard, had threatened to immobilise her.

So, at the end of a week in which the entire Martone family was left feeling wounded and silent, Rose was at Lucy's house. And here, on the news, on the television that sat in the corner of Lucy's living room, Rose recognised something else from the past—the old kitchen block Lucy and she used to work in. She remembered the uniform she used to wear, the gloves, the apron, the pinafore that held her body tightly in place, the stray hairs falling from the boundaries of her hairnet, and the thought of all that made her smile.

There used to be a garden, right behind where that razor wire was now. The New Australians used to help grow herbs and tomatoes and pumpkins there for the kitchen staff to use in their cooking. She still remembered the Spanish and Polish and Greek words for things. *Pepino, ziemniak, vasilikós*. She would trade a word in English for a word in another tongue when she picked things with the residents. Cucumber for *pepino*, basil for *vasilikós*. That's where she'd met Antonio.

'How do you say this?' he would ask her, holding up a potato or a sprig of mint.

'Potato.'

She would watch him think about it, the word, watch him rolling it over on his tongue before he released it from his mouth fully formed, 'potato'.

Now, the camera cut to a shot of three men on the roof of that building she remembered so fondly. It went closer, closer, until it showed their dark hair and large begging eyes. They sat cross-legged in faded T-shirts and jeans, their fat lips sewn together with dark thread. Now, the camera moved out again to a long shot of the buildings that had been burned down in the riots of previous months. Now, it focused on a child standing there, looking up expressionless at the men on the roof. Now, the camera took a close-up of the razor wire bent like a corkscrewed silver earring. Now, it was focusing on the pink-glossed lips of the reporter outside. She flicked her blond hair and raised her eyebrows from the television screen as if to say, 'what are we supposed to do with all of this?'

'Sometimes I can't believe that place is the same place we worked in.' Rose had said it as a thought but somehow it had come out of her mouth. Lucy was purse-lipped. Her butter hair fell around her face as she lifted her teacup up to take a sip.

'It's almost not the same place. The Nissen huts are gone. There's only a few of those old brick buildings that used to be around in our time.'

Rose watched Lucy sip her tea and thought of her back then, cigarette in hand, stirring a pot of something in the kitchen of the hostel, wearing her sex on the outside for all to see.

'Do you remember that family, the Spanish one that was in all the photos? That woman, what was her name? She looked like Audrey Hepburn with pinned-back dark glossy curls and all her children in starched white pinafores?'

'Those ones? Of course. They were in everything. Everything. All the brochures they put out, whenever they needed something in the newspaper. They were the most beautiful-looking lot. They were right up there with those cowboys on the "Australia: Land of Tomorrow!" posters. I guess that's how they got everyone here, with promises of good-looking strangers. Like a nightclub.'

Villawood was the start of Rose's new life. To her it was the opposite of a nightclub—more like a village somewhere in a European town far away. Compared to Surry Hills, the place seemed endless and green, rural almost, a calm blue-green whirl. It wasn't people on top of people, crammed up in terraces and apartment blocks. Even with all the people that were there, there was more of a sense of order. The Nissen huts sat in neat rows, the migrants stood in straight lines, there was no noise after nine.

And then what? Rose watched as Lucy yawned and turned the volume up on the television. 'It was different then,' she said.

'Not so different.' Lucy replied. 'Remember? There were protests back then too. Remember the residents went on hunger strikes, same as they do now. They had the same strategy as the government does today, you tell people where they can and can't go, you don't let them cook their own food, you take away their choices, you make it difficult for them to find their own home somewhere, you don't allow them any responsibility, you just tell them to wait for something that you won't explain or define and you don't tell them how long that waiting will be. And then you make them wait and wait some more until they start to break down and go mad and they sew their lips together because there's nothing else they have left and then we put them on the TV knowing they look a bit like Frankenstein and that lets everyone turn away because they don't look quite human and we allow ourselves to forget that people from other places are human too.'

Outside they heard the screeching of tires again. This time neither of them got up to look out the window and see what had happened. Rose looked at Lucy in a sideways kind of way that said, 'I am looking at you but I don't want you to notice.' This was one of those moments when she was reminded that Lucy always seemed more worldly than her, like she had spent so much longer thinking about the ways that the universe worked, and had reached all her conclusions a long time ago.

And to confirm what Rose was thinking Lucy added, 'That's what pushes people over the limit, when they are pushed back from adulthood and squeezed into some kind of juvenile form.'

But Rose looked at the people behind the razor wire and

knew that everything had been different back then. She knew
this for sure. She had been there in that kitchen, in that garden.

'But we wanted them back then,' she said.

'Wanted them and in another way we didn't want them.'

'But we didn't lock them up. They came and went.'

Briefly, Lucy turned her head from the television and faced
Rose, a look of quizzical irritation on her face. 'But you weren't
there. Not really. Not *in* there. Ask Antonio, he knows what
I'm talking about.'

Rose felt jealous—not because of any shared devotion
between Antonio and Lucy, but because they shared this piece
of history of which she wasn't a part. There were people who
had been in there and those who had not. She recognised
something, a kind of knowing between Lucy and her husband,
that she had never recognised before. Sometimes she forgot
the place was also the start of Lucy's new life when her family
had arrived from Poland, just like it was for Rose, but in a way
that was not at all the same.

On the television a man behind the razor wire turned and
faced Rose, looked at her directly in the eyes and said, 'If you
Australians think that I am an animal, then tell me that I am an
animal so that I come to think of myself as an animal and don't
expect to be treated like a human.'

Rose had to get out for some air.

Outside her house looked unfamiliar again. On the pavement there was the refuse left by people who had come to
watch the show that was her current life: a Pauline Hanson
poster ripped in two, a beer can, a white plastic chair.

Something she is sure was true: when she was about twenty,
nineteen maybe, she had sneaked into Antonio's section of one
of the Nissen huts and got caught there in a storm. Everything
in those huts was bigger, louder, hotter than it was on the outside, so that when it rained it was like being trapped in the eye

of a tornado. She had sat on his bed while Antonio sat on the chair beside it. Behind him, the curtain that separated his space from the man next door shook in rhythm to the rain landing on the uninsulated tin roof above it. They had sat in silence. The awkwardness of a young woman sitting alone on a foreigner's bed hanging in the air until a flash of lightning through the doorway turned the outside into a brief, vivid white. Then they both started to laugh. It was Rose first, mostly because of the look of terror in Antonio's eyes. It startled her. The nervous laughter came straight from the awkwardness sitting deep down in her guts. The lightning might have been the punchline for some kind of long and complicated joke no one understood. When they were through laughing, they talked about the future, about the possibility of having a future together in some place that was not here, and for the first time the storybook idea of it became something that was almost real. After the storm had passed Rose had sneaked back to the kitchen. Later, they would learn that the lightning had struck one of the other Nissen huts, sending electric currents across the inside of its roof and causing a spooked young woman to run, scandalously half-dressed, out into the rain.

Now she walked over to her house slowly, alone. The lights from the apartment building next door lit up the empty rooms that hovered in the skyline above. They were like spotlights from a movie set, lighting up the darkness on the main stage that was her home. For a moment she could imagine what it would be like to watch this whole story unfolding from her television set, in some other space somewhere that felt more like home.

24.

T he Martone women, they were slightly unreal. There was something about them that was never grounded in the actual world as everyone else experienced it. Of late, Francis had been wondering if there was something more wrong with them than whatever was wrong with his father.

Today, he had escaped from his mum standing on a milk crate at the side of their house so that she could peer through the window of her own home from the outside, from his father sitting at the kitchen table nodding attentively to a guy who looked like a skinhead, from a giant boat painted on the concrete of his front yard, and from people hanging out on the pavement in front of his house who wouldn't move to let him back his car out so that he could get to work on time. And then, as if things couldn't get any shittier, as if the universe had arrived to tell him in no uncertain terms that he was definitely its biggest loser, he'd arrived at his sister's house only to be greeted with the shocking fact that his sister, of all people, got laid much more often than he did.

Francis was in the living room downstairs, waiting for her to finish her business upstairs with someone Clare's flatmate referred to as 'the guy who comes to hang out in Clare's bedroom from time to time'—wink wink—but he was not really interested in explaining it all to Francis; he was busy staring at the television where the face of the umpire who was apparently ripping off his team kept flashing up to a lot of angry booing.

Francis sank himself into the couch and read the posters on

the wall. The place was a strange cross of bachelor pad with female uni student share house. There was a Man U poster, signed and framed, and a set of matching orange posters from something called The Best Books series. The boring-looking heads of people no one cared about stared down at him as he read the quotes that summed them up: 'What a woman needs is a room of her own'. Yep, what a man needed was a home of his own.

With the difference in their ages, he'd never really gotten to know his sister that well. He'd been eleven when she'd left home at eighteen to live in what his father had called 'The Commune' someplace near to where she studied. He still remembered the fights back then about her leaving, and then the fights when she did come home to visit with dirty hair and no bra and all that talk of politics and things his father didn't agree with and he didn't understand. It was like all of a sudden she'd become cool and adultlike and she had all these friends. Not like before, when she was in high school and he understood her a little bit better as being like one of the girls in his class who hung out with the other kids who were only stuck together by the fact that they were all losers. He remembered her as hanging out back then with other girls whose hair was too frizzy. They had sat in her bedroom on a Saturday night, eating peanut-butter crackers till the gunk got stuck in their braces, and they'd read each other love poems and sing love songs like they were written especially for them. Clare had been geeky, nerdy. She'd lived in books and she quoted things at the family all the time, as if all those writers could stand in for her own lack of personality. He'd always felt a certain superiority over her, even when he was eleven, purely because he wasn't totally socially inept.

But now she was a different kind of beast. She had style, she went to nice bars. She'd developed the ability to hold an actual conversation with people. She possibly wasn't even a teacher anymore. She had sex. Who knew when that had all started? He hadn't been paying attention and something had happened while he'd been looking away.

He heard footsteps coming down the stairs and looked up to see his sister, but instead there was a tall thin guy with messed up red hair. He looked like he belonged in some kind of 80s rock band. He wore a faded shirt with a picture of the earth and the words, 'It's getting hot in here!' written underneath. He paused to tie up the laces of his Converse at the bottom of the stairs and nodded at Francis and the flatmate sitting there on the couch.

'What's the score?'

'Two-nil.'

'Better luck next time,' he said and walked himself straight out the door.

Without breaking his eyes from the television, Clare's flatmate said, 'Give it a few minutes. She'll come down for toast and a bottle of wine and you can catch her before she disappears upstairs again. Best kind of flatmate. Goes to work. Comes home. Disappears into her room. I call her the phantom in stilettos.'

And sure enough, ten minutes later Clare emerged down the stairs. Not a hair out of place. She was looking straight forward at the wall like she was thinking of something else until she caught Francis' eyes and stopped.

'Oh shit,' she said, and nothing else, before pausing for a long time there, holding the railing. 'What are you doing here?'

Francis wasn't sure by the tone of her voice if that meant 'what are you doing here?' as in he wasn't wanted, or 'what are you doing here?' as in she was surprised to see him, or 'what are you doing here?' as in she was glad that he had finally come.

'I was just around. Had to get out of the house. You know.

All sorts of crazy there. Thought things would be less crazy here.' He couldn't help smiling and he knew it was that smile that made her turn red underneath her high cheekbones.

'How about we get out of here?' she said. 'Go get a drink or something. My shout.'

'Sure. Whatever. Sounds good.'

Outside, Cleveland Street was starting to get busy, even on a Wednesday night. People were dressed up and ready to go. Clare took him to that kind of bar in the city where you pay too much to sit on mismatching chairs and drink cocktails from old jam jars and tomato soup cans.

'Nice,' he said when she sat down at their table with a bunch of tacos in a plastic basket and two Bloody Marys in old soup cans.

'Nice,' he said again because he didn't really know where to start just being out, being casual like this with a stranger he was related to. He lit a cigarette, stirred his drink with the celery stick that came with it.

'You think it's wanky.'

'Yeah.' But he quickly added, 'It's nice too, you know, to be here with you.'

She nodded. He was always better at being nice than she was. He watched her look away at the couple sitting next to them, and thought for the first time that she was actually quite beautiful. She had their mother's strong jaw and smooth peachy skin.

She looked back at him, tapped her nails against the table, looked a bit like she had something real important she was going to say.

'What?' he said, after waiting too long for her to speak.

'Okay. Shut up.'

'I didn't say anything.'

'You did. You said everything with your eyes.'

'With my eyes, hey?' he replied. He didn't look at her. He

watched the Nikes on the feet of someone sitting next to them and he smiled because she was obviously still uncomfortable about the guy who came out of her bedroom. This shit was funny but he knew that he wasn't permitted to laugh.

'I don't care, Clare. I don't care about that guy and whatever you do, you know, to entertain yourself in your own spare time.'

'He's not . . . ' Clare began to say and then dropped it.

'He's whatever. I don't care. I really don't. I am kind of jealous you pick up more than me though.'

She ran her hand through her hair and slouched back into her chair like she could relax now that topic of conversation was over.

'Guess you've got bigger things to worry about, living in that house.'

'It's your house too. They're your fucked-up parents too.'

'Yeah. Guess so.' She looked tired. Distracted.

He waited for her to have more to offer but that was it. Her mobile phone rang and she said, 'Sorry, I've got to get this.'

She answered the phone, broke into a smile and a pepped-up voice like she was putting on a show for the person who couldn't see her at the other end of the line, then walked off to the opposite side of the bar so she could have her conversation away from him.

Left on his own, he drank his drink and then hers, ate all the tacos and then went to the bar for another round. He wanted real drinks in real beer bottles and he had to wait too long to order them so he started looking at the posters behind the bar where Buffy the Vampire Slayer was saying 'Once More With Feeling!' according to the speech bubble that hung out of her mouth. The place sucked.

When he was finally in possession of two beers he found himself back at their table alone again. He watched his sister flick her hair in the corner and laugh into the phone and he wondered if she gave two shits about everything that was happening.

When she finally returned to the table he had finished his beer and started in on the one he had bought for her. She was laughing quietly to herself when she put her phone back in her bag and finally looked at him again like he had missed out on some great joke.

'Sorry, sorry. Just a work thing. You know.'

By this time the alcohol had got stuck into him and he didn't feel like being so gentle anymore. 'And where do you work?'

'Sorry?'

'Where do you work? Dad went down to your school to visit you the other day and you weren't there. None of us can work out what you're doing. You haven't even told us.'

'It's complicated.'

'Why? What's so complicated? Dad's complicated, Mum's complicated. Changing jobs is not so complicated. He's pissed, you know, that you've shut him out. Shut everyone out. Do you even know what it's like in that place? You just show up and tell Mum what to do and then you piss off in some guy's van. Dad's completely lost it. He's high on morphine, or he's got dementia or he's just batshit crazy or maybe he's just like a really hurt, pathetic human being, or maybe a scarier thought—he knows exactly what he's doing and he's doing it anyway. I don't know and there's these guys that keep coming around, they're even crazier than him and they're using him as some sort of poster boy for their cause. And where are you, Clare? Where are you?'

He watched her take a deep breath, watched her thinking of the right words. Then she said in a slow, steady voice, 'I do. I do care. It's just hard . . .'

He drank the rest of the second beer in three big mouthfuls and looked her straight in the eyes before walking out.

'Once more with feeling, Clare. Once more with feeling.'

25

Once again, Clare returned to her childhood home and there were strangers on her lawn. When Paul found somewhere three blocks away to park, they realised there was the problem of what to do with the paint. Clare turned around in the front seat and looked at it sitting there in the back of the van, all four two-litre cans of white.

'You can't exactly just wander down the street holding so much paint can you?' She hadn't thought about that part, about how ridiculous it would look, and she certainly hadn't thought about the people who would be there to witness it.

'Yeah, actually, it's all a bit too obvious looking.' Paul ran his hands in quiet contemplation through the hair hanging over his forehead. 'What if someone tries to stop us, like that crazy guy with the megaphone.'

'I don't know.' Clare was thinking more about such a public act of shaming. Of course, she'd had disagreements with her father before, but throwing paint on the front yard of his house in front of so many people suddenly felt like something from *The Scarlet Letter*, as if she were the moral police, there to cast him out of the community.

'Okay,' she said, 'how about we just walk over, without the paint, see how things are?'

They got out of the van and walked up to where the people were milling around on the footpath. This time the crowd was split in two. On one side, a grey-haired man with a megaphone and his crowd of neatly dressed middle-aged people and skinheads. On the other side were scruffy young white kids who looked like clichéd versions of university students, and a few of the local boys Clare recognised from around the way. Not doing the best job of holding the two sides apart were two police officers, who narrated what was going on over their walkie-talkies as though the people they were talking about couldn't understand what they were saying. Both sides hung back, away from each other, except for the smallest of the skinheads and the largest of the local boys.

One of the skinheads grabbed the megaphone from where the grey-haired man had momentarily left it on the ground to take a sip of water. He rushed at one of the local boys, a massive Pasifika guy. Clare had seen this man heaps over the years. He must have been maybe mid- to late-twenties. Clare used to see him with his mates at the park watching the sun set from the park bench. She remembered him mostly because he always looked so much like he was content to just be where he was, enjoying things with his friends. Maybe his name was Pat. That's how he'd introduced himself to her once when they'd been stuck on a bus together and he'd recognised her from the neighbourhood.

The skinhead rushed at him with his megaphone, shoved it right up near his face and yelled, 'We have the right to decide who comes to this country. We have the right.'

But before he could go on, Pat grabbed that megaphone back off him. He fell over and Pat stood over him, not touching him. Pat was huge in comparison to the skinhead, darker. Pat leant down closer, closer, with the megaphone held up to his mouth and Clare noticed that the skinhead had black tears tattooed down the right side of his face.

'Look at you—you little anorexic fuck,' Pat spat into the microphone. 'You fucking dog, you're the hard man in the crew, are ya?'

And then the police were on him, grabbing at the megaphone,

but Pat made sure that he got the last word in, 'Look at me. Look at me! Welcome to the future!' he yelled.

The police grabbed at him and he stretched his big black arms into the air and shook them like he was in the audience at a Beastie Boys concert, and the uni students clapped and the row of elderly gentlemen standing off in the foreground held their Pauline Hanson posters higher up in solidarity with the skinhead's plight.

In the front window she could see her father peeking out through the venetians like he did when they were children, and there was an unexpected noise on the street. She felt Paul standing too close to her as they leaned against the fence, and she thought of Francis at the pub, when he had asked her where she worked now. She felt her father's gaze on her skin.

'It'll be dark soon. We could come back then. Maybe then there won't be so many people. Maybe we could paint it over in the dark.' Paul was staring hard at the image of the boat. 'I didn't think . . . I don't think, looking at it now, that I expected to find it so, you know, like an accusation against me personally or something . . . I don't know, I feel like I can't look up, like people are staring at me.'

Clare scanned the crowd. On both sides there looked like there were people who weren't exactly white. No one appeared to be staring at Paul, but maybe she just couldn't see what he saw, standing there in a different skin.

'Why don't we go for a walk? It'll be dark soon. We could get something to eat, walk along the river or something. Come back when it's dark.'

Paul nodded his head but didn't move. He looked like he was fixed in the boat's gaze. She gave his elbow a little squeeze and started to walk out ahead of him, down the hill towards the river. A misty kind of rain began to fall. Away from the house, the streets felt still and quiet. Paul walked looking down at his feet.

'My first protest,' he said. 'And I bowed out pretty quickly.'

'Your first? What do they do with you at university these days?' she said in a mocking tone that wasn't at all convincing. Her head was off somewhere else. 'Don't think I did much at uni, besides read books and go to protests.'

'Really? Can't imagine it. You being like that. You seem so not willing to fight now.'

She started again, 'I was like crazy busy with self-invention. I joined all those anti-nuclear marches and spent the night chained to a chair inside the Vice Chancellor's office. I got kind of stuck in this vortex of radicalism. It sucks you in. Mostly, the social side of it. I was just like awkward and book-ish and I didn't know how to talk to people, so it worked for me. You know, people shouting slogans all the time. I didn't have to talk and nobody noticed me, but I got to be in this big crowd of people. I could convince myself that I was never lonely, but I was always alone. I'm not sure if anyone really even knew I existed.'

Richard had shown her that she really did exist back then, ten years ago when they had more of a relationship than just having sex at her place. These days, when she and Richard were lying in bed, she'd think about him back then, when he had seemed to take up so much more space. One day when they were in university she had run into Richard in Newtown, and he had abruptly held up his paint-stained palms in front of her and ordered her to stop, and because she was so drawn to the frantic face he made sometimes, she had done as she was told.

'You've got to come back to my house,' Richard had said, and she'd thought he wanted to do the same things to her that he'd done after they'd drunk too much the previous week, but when she got there, there were half a dozen people in his back-yard with tubs of paint and rolls of cloth and shirts and a screen printing contraption. The grass was freckled in all the primary colours. There were large posters hanging on the back fence that said things like 'Every Race *Is* Equal—Blainey' and 'I'm not swamped by Asians'. Richard had stopped the radio that was playing in the boombox in the middle of the lawn and put in a tape of a man who was speaking in an animated voice about extremes. 'You cannot go from being all white to being all Asian. It's too extreme—we've opened the floodgates.'

Richard spoke over the top, 'You've heard of this man? Professor Racist Blainey?'

She had, vaguely, but she hadn't gotten her head around it yet. She'd just gotten her head around the anti-nuclear movement, all that stuff about land rights and nuclear war and vegetables near Chernobyl that glowed in the dark when you pulled them from the ground, and now she saw that everything was changing, that the new issues were all about identity and who had the right to belong. She was caught off guard, but she'd agreed to go to the protest he was planning anyway. Something about Richard inspired patronage, as if by helping him you were helping a multitude of other people who really wanted to be saved, just by him. That she'd never ended up going to the protest somehow mattered a lot less to her in retrospect.

And now, in the present, Paul was shaking his head and saying, 'I can't really see you being that way.'

'Different life. No use to me now.'

They walked, and things between them became quiet again, but in a way that felt comfortable to Clare, quiet in a way that said that maybe they were thinking about things they were not entirely secure with, but they were safe with each other, just walking past all those houses with their weatherboard and sandstone and brick. The houses were painted the colours of suburban kitchens: eggshell, beige, pale yellow.

Now, they'd come to the upper part of the Parramatta River

and were walking towards the asylum. It was starting to get dark and with the soft rain the landscape was turning into one of those kinds of evenings here that she missed, now that she lived in the city. On evenings like this, the mist rolled out over the river and covered everything. It formed on the east side up the hill where she grew up, and then it swept its way through the mangroves and past the early evening joggers along the riverside.

She imagined the fog moving through the mangroves and out over the place where the salt water met the fresh water of the Parramatta River and those early explorers could take their boats no further. She could see it moving over images of the Aboriginal warrior Pemulwuy who chased all those invaders and their boats back out towards the ocean, and could picture it drifting its way under Lennox Bridge past the moss-covered hulls and petrified wooden rudders of boats that got stranded here two hundred years ago, then squeezing itself between the squat rectangles of '60s brick apartment blocks where it bothered the bats that hung there all day, lifeless in the trees. Now she watched as it picked itself up again until it got to the end of the river, where it laid its opaque hands over the buildings where so many people had been locked up or had gone insane, not necessarily in that order. This was why that mist was Parramatta and why Parramatta was the nation, because there were so many things hidden out there on the water.

And now that mist was hiding Clare and Paul, and a question about paint was hanging unsaid between them. She looked up and saw the bats upside down in the trees like fruit gone dark and rotten. There were people who lived in the bushes below the trees who came out at night, like the bats, and then there were the ghosts that locals, from time to time, would claim to see as well—the translucent girls in the pinafores they had made them wear in the home for girls, the body of a man in chains floating down the river.

And then it popped from Clare's mouth before she had a chance to stop it, 'You're the only person I can be myself with.'

'Why?' He seemed startled.

'I don't know. I guess I don't worry what you think about me.'

'Maybe you should.'

She looked at Paul. She wasn't sure what he meant by delivering a statement so matter-of-factly but she knew that he was thinking by the way he looked away.

'Maybe,' she said.

They kept walking up to the grounds of the old asylum. Paul read the new signs on all the old buildings as they passed without expression: Methadone Clinic I, Methadone Clinic II, Youth Rehabilitation, Women's Services, Multicultural Addiction Services. She'd always loved the asylum. Always. In a romantic kind of way, because it made her feel as though she was wandering through a Gothic novel, all that crumbling sandstone and the untrimmed vines creeping across abandoned chapels, that feeling of menace everywhere as though someone might leap out from one of the buildings at any moment and crawl into your body.

Clare looked at the roof tiles of the main building, the Female Factory, where they locked up all those women. The tiles in the entranceway to the building always brought her back to the facts of the place as it really was. She had seen a woman talk once in a festival at Parramatta Park. She'd been put into the girls' home there, and she talked about how, sometime in the 1960s, she and a bunch of primary school-aged girls who were in there too had climbed up onto the roof and torn the roof tiles off one by one, throwing them at the guards on the ground because no one listened to them. And then, the woman explained, they'd been made to sleep under that roof with its missing tiles all winter, fat streams of water pouring in through the holes of the roof. The girls were told the roof would not be fixed until they agreed to apologise, but they had refused. They got wet. That's what a protest was.

She was about to tell Paul this story but he spoke first.

'We don't say anything.' It sounded like a statement he'd been considering for a long time.

'What do you want me to say?'

'No not you. Us. *Our* generation of boat people, about *these* boat people. Actually you too, everyone. You don't say anything either. I'm not even sure if you care at all, other than finding the whole thing a nuisance. You know my community, we were refugees too. But, you know, *not like them*, as my mother would say.'

Clare was looking at the roof of the old Female Factory where the bats had begun to fly overhead. The setting sun behind the old asylum made it light up like it was on fire behind the mist.

She had something she'd considered too. 'What if nobody owes anybody anything?' She said it to the fog.

26.

Her mother hadn't wanted her to hang out with 'those Surry Hills girls', so she'd stayed in the terrace most of the time, behind that window she was standing in front of now, the house someone had painted in tasteful blues and greens. Back when Rose's mother rented the front room, she'd spent her days as a teenager sitting on the edge of the bed they shared, looking out into the grey of the street.

She'd come to Surry Hills to see Clare, but she hadn't made it to her house. Rose loved her daughter, but sometimes she didn't like her very much. She was always telling Rose what to do, not listening, just talking. It was like this with everyone in Rose's life, always, even way back then, she thought, as she stared through the window to where someone had arranged old floral china plates on the wall in some fashion she supposed was meant to be tasteful, in the way that young people these days found old things at the Salvos interesting.

When they'd lived there, the whole terrace had had a hospital-like quality; there was always the smell of harsh chemicals lining the inside of your nose. On her mother's nervous days she had cleaned the place like she was possessed. She would scrub the paint right off the walls so that things looked dingy and grey. All the boarders knew if you smelled bleach, Rose's mum wasn't having a good day. And Rose knew that she couldn't go anywhere, couldn't leave her.

That heat. Rose wasn't sure why she always remembered it being so hot in the terrace. It must have been cold in the winter too, but when she looked at it now, all she could recall was the heat. She was always on the verge of suffocation, always had too many clothes on; those thick brown winter stockings and twin sets, all that hair pinned back neatly, the A-line skirts that sucked everything in and held it in place.

Her mother had wanted out of Surry Hills, out to any-where, that's what everyone seemed to be doing after the war; half of Cleveland Street got up and moved to the safety of the suburbs, but they couldn't afford it. Instead they stayed home, her mother cleaning, sewing clothes for people by hand. Rose went to school and later to work at the grocery store, but she was always home long before the dark set in.

Inside the terrace, the dark would arrive through the win-dows. Her mother would sew in the lamplight without looking up. Rose had stayed locked up inside herself, sitting with her mother and the crackly talk of the radio. Nothing much to mark the days as being different from one another: A warm glass of milk before bed and the dishes washed, the floors scrubbed clean and her mother snoring softly under the blankets.

Rose remembers when she was a child, her mother had still been waiting, watching out that window for the Japanese to invade after they sunk those submarines in the nearby harbour during the war, but they never came back. Later, the Italians came instead, and then the Greeks and the Lebanese Christians and the everything elses. The men wore their best pants and their only collared shirts of an evening, and they hung out on street corners in shiny black shoes, smoking ciga-rettes, leaning up against lampposts, always talking. To Rose they reminded her now of the extras in *Casablanca*. They brought their loud sing-song voices and their big hands and all those 'r's rolling off their tongues like molasses.

'Stay away from the windows,' her mother would urge. 'They'll see you.' But Rose was never really clear on what could happen if she was seen, and besides, there was nowhere to go.

The streets weren't safe anymore, according to her mother and everyone else. So Rose sat at the windows imagining she was Audrey Hepburn in *Roman Holiday*, just waiting to get out and explore the new world unnoticed.

But the heat. The heat. She'd stayed all locked up, watching the New Australians from the window. Everywhere you looked back then, there was something you'd never seen before, a brightly embroidered skirt, fat loaves of hard brown Italian bread. Next to the new arrivals, Rose had thought all the Australians looked tired and thin. In the early morning, before dawn, before her mother woke, she would sit on her windowsill and watch the men and women walking up to the factories, brown paper bags in their hands.

The morning her mother died she must have been hanging there in the laundry for such a long time. Rose had been sitting on the windowsill, watching a man with the darkest, curliest hair she had ever seen leaning up against the wall of the apartment block across the street, wondering if she could get her mum to take her to the pictures for her nineteenth birthday.

Now, in her reflection in the window, Rose looked like she was going to burst out of her own body. She could be at Clare's place in less than ten minutes but she didn't want to go. The memory of that heat made her yearn for different things.

27

W hat Antonio had gotten himself into here went further back in time than he could imagine. It started way back in 1914 when John Solomon's father George Solomon wrote 'Greece' in that little space next to 'Country of Origin' on his application for Australian citizenship. 'Lebanese-Syrian' wasn't going to cut it until the White Australia Policy was dropped sixty years later. A journalist had found George's own words in the National Archives. 'It is a true fact. I was born in Aleppo in Syria, on 18 February 1888, and the other application which was made in 1916 last, it is not the correct one, and you know it for a fact there were no Asiatics allowed to become naturalised unless he made an application and showed he was born in some part of Europe, and for that reason I got told to say so, and I do not know any difference it made in saying it.'

This morning, Antonio and Skinhead Bruce with all the tears tattooed down his face were sitting at John Solomon's kitchen table. The spirit of George, otherwise known as the King of the Riverina because he came to Australia with not a penny and ended up owning most of Main Street, was hanging over the scene like a bad smell. Skinhead Bruce, who had just this morning been put in his place again over the stealing of the megaphone at the protest in front of Antonio's house, had talked about George, as he often did when he wasn't getting enough attention, or when things weren't going his way.

'Sol-eeh-man,' Skinhead Bruce said, 'isn't a very European-sounding name.'

John Solomon wasn't going to dignify the comment by giving it much attention. 'It's pronounced Sol-o-mn.'

Skinhead Bruce sat back in his chair, crossed his arms over his chest like a petulant teenager; in fact as Antonio looked at him more closely he thought he couldn't be that far off a teenager in age. He was early- to mid-twenties, scrawny, the kind of guy who finds it impossible to grow facial hair. Skinhead Bruce looked at John Solomon again and said, more loudly this time and at a closer distance to his face, 'Did your father pronounce it that way? George Sol-eeh-man. I read about him in another newspaper article again. Says old George was a Leb from Syria. 'Snot in Europe is it, Syria?'

'My grandfather was from Greece. It says so on his naturalisation certificate. I sent it to the newspaper.'

'Greeks, Arabs all foreign though ain't they?'

'No. Greeks and Arabs are a different species.'

Antonio continued to fold pamphlets while Skinhead Bruce and John Solomon argued. He placed the pamphlets in a neat stack beside him and read the bolded quotes: 'Today's invasions don't have to be military. They can be of diseases; they can be of unwanted migrants. —Solicitor General of Australia, David Bennett'. He was listening to John Solomon and Skinhead Bruce and he was not. Lately, he felt more than ever that he was walking through a dream he couldn't wake from. It was hard for his conscious self to stay there in the room, to remain focused, to listen.

Antonio remembered the Arab men on the building site. They could have been Greek, or maybe Italian like him. A couple of them, he'd never gotten their names, came around to see him at the hospital after the accident in which Nico had died. They had brought him biscuits drenched in honey. Now, they didn't come around to see him anymore.

Antonio knew he had just missed some important part of the conversation. John Solomon's hand reached up, not far from Antonio's nose, and slapped Skinhead Bruce hard on the cheek. Skinhead Bruce stood up, grabbed a chair as he left and threw it against the wall. The smashing sound made Antonio snap back to the here and now. His leg ached under the table.

One thing that Antonio understood clearly at this moment was that the mention of his father made John Solomon angry. He took two more of the A4 sheets from the pile on the table and folded them quickly in an irritated manner. Antonio kept on folding and did not say anything until John Solomon looked up and glared at him.

'This is it,' he said. 'This is important work we are doing. Information, knowledge, you know that is the most powerful thing. That's why I've spent so much of my time reading since I was a little boy, finding out about the world. That's why I did my PhD in political science, because I wanted to know how the world worked and now, we have the opportunity—no, the privilege—to share that information with others.'

John Solomon stood up like one of those politicians at question time who had become so fed up with the opposition that there was nothing he could do but stand up and shout over the bodies of people who were clearly much more stupid than himself. He was getting fired up now. 'You know, way back in university when I started the National Front it was our graffiti and literature displayed on walls and street poles that got Blainey thinking about the multicultural and immigration issue.' He stopped speaking abruptly and clenched his teeth, like he was trying to steady himself before he got up and punched everyone out. He looked at the statue of Ned Kelly.

A driver in one of the trucks on the Princes Highway pressed down on his brakes and the sound came screeching through the house. Ned Kelly shook slightly on his base, as if he might jump up at any minute and join the conversation.

John Solomon piled the folded brochures into the cardboard box on the table and told Antonio, 'You're doing a good job.' He looked at him for a long time like he wanted to make sure that Antonio knew he meant it.

It was time to leave. Antonio knew this by now. There was always a strict formality to the way that John Solomon did things, an invisible schedule that must be followed. Lunch was always at twelve, afternoon tea at three. John Solomon required constant refreshment. The working bees ended at five. John Solomon needed time alone to work on his big ideas in the semi-dark of that terrace, with his notebook and pen and a thoughtful look on his face.

When Antonio walked through the backyard to where his car was parked out in the lane, he heard noises coming from the shed.

It was large, and sturdy-looking for a shed in the backyard of an old terrace in the inner west. It was made of galvanised steel and had a large lock on the door, which Antonio noticed was unlocked and hanging off the slightly open door. More curious to Antonio, though, was the fact that John Solomon didn't really have much of a yard to speak of, just some patchy grass, a strip of concrete that didn't require seeds, or potting mix or weed removers or lawn mowers—the types of things you keep in a shed.

From the inside of the shed he heard another thump and suddenly the light switched on and seeped out underneath the door. When he opened it he could see Skinhead Bruce, unmistakably with his tattoo-teary face grabbing things off a shelf and throwing them to the ground. When Antonio opened the door further and stood at the entrance he could see what Skinhead Bruce was throwing—thick hard-backed books in solid colours, the type you find in the reference sections of libraries. The entire shed was lined with shelves holding mostly books in neat rows piled from the floor to the ceiling, with the exception of the back wall where there were stacks of pamphlets and posters and neatly folded flags. Skinhead Bruce pulled a row of the books out until the back wall was revealed. The books seemed huge against his thin limbs moving back and forth across the shed but he must have been stronger than he looked because it didn't seem difficult for him. Antonio watched Skinhead Bruce feel around with his hands as if there might be something that his eyes had missed.

It was a few minutes before he acknowledged Antonio's presence by giving him a sour look and turning back to the work at hand.

'You gonna help or what? Just stand there doing nothin' like that prick. Fucking King Solomon.'

The motion of his arms reaching back and forth, of books flying from one side of the shed and landing on the other made Antonio feel as though he were in a washing machine. He sat before he could fall over on a cardboard box by the entrance. He didn't know what he was sitting on but he was glad it held his weight. He leant forward, rested his face in his hands and tried to concentrate on stopping the world from spinning.

'It's here,' Skinhead Bruce was saying. Thump. Thump. Antonio could feel the vibrations of the books bounding against the wall behind him.

'Motherfucker.' Thump. Thump.

Antonio lifted his head to see if Skinhead Bruce had found the thing he was looking for but clearly he had not. He was resting his forehead against the shelf.

'What are you looking for?'

'His gun.'

Antonio could feel his palms start to sweat. He didn't know if he should move. 'Why?'

'I'm going to kill him.'

This last declaration wasn't said with much emotion. Skinhead Bruce's voice had gone flat and he was standing there hunched over slightly, as though he had thrown all his conviction out with the books on the ground. He sat next to Antonio and caught his breath. Skinhead Bruce had a meanness, something deep down that was always there.

'What makes you think he's got a gun anyway?'

Antonio doubted its existence. From what he had seen of John Solomon he seemed more of a 'the pen is mightier than the sword' type.

'Well, before he became a pussy, he was arrested for giving a guy a gun to shoot up the house of those Muslims that run Lakemba Mosque. Motherfucker says he's all about books and knowledge and shit but really he just wants to shoot people back to where they belong.'

'Shoot them.' Antonio repeated. It was more of a statement than a question. He couldn't begin to get his head around all that. He thought of Matilda and Joe painting stars on houses at night, and the young guys in lowered cars who threw paint bombs at his house; he thought of his daughter with that Asian boy standing on the pavement with the protesters mocking him, and the construction workers next door calling out all the time and laughing when he looked their way, and he thought *a gun*! That was something that made you take a person seriously, and then he thought *no*.

'No gun.' Antonio said, more as a way of steadying his own desires than as a reply to Skinhead Bruce who had begun to crack his knuckles as though he was gearing up for a fight.

'I think we should get out of here now before John Solomon sees us.'

'Couldn't give a shit,' Skinhead Bruce replied and it was probably true, but also, things were over and Skinhead Bruce seemed to know it. They left the shed and walked out to the back alleyway. Antonio was tired. His whole body began to ache. When he got into the car and rolled down the window Skinhead Bruce's head was suddenly beside his. Up this close

Antonio could see that his skin was pockmarked and flaky. There were small beads of sweat forming at the top of his dry lips.

'I could get you one, you know,' he said, wiping the sweat off with the back of his hand.

'What?

'A gun.'

'Why?'

'For your own protection.'

28

Charbel's apartment looked exactly the way you would expect the apartment of a 24-year-old male who had recently moved out of home to look: sparse on practical and also ornamental things. There were no saucepans or framed photographs, just that one couch he'd got from someone, a bed, the television on top of an esky, too many odd pieces of worn clothing on the bathroom floor.

Francis was kind of living there and kind of not. He had slept over one night and he came sometimes in the afternoons to get a break from his own home on the days when he felt like he might just up and explode. His home wasn't his home anymore. It was filled with silence on the inside, and there was too much noise on the outside. His mum and sister, where were they? He'd been left to carry it all. And *he* was meant to be the irresponsible one.

It was all getting freakier than he'd ever thought it could. He'd walked through the garage last night and almost split in two when he'd seen his dad with that gun. His dad was just standing there, just like that, turning it over in his hand. He'd held it like it was enormous and heavy, and even in that shadowy space Francis could see that there were connections being made: his dad was thinking about something he shouldn't, maybe about the protesters or the boats or his own diminished life. When Francis had leant up against the creaky door too hard, his dad got startled and dropped the gun and it broke into four different pieces on the ground.

They'd both laughed so hard Francis had pissed his pants a

little with the relief of it all. He recognised it later picking those plastic pieces up off the ground. Francis had bought the gun himself at the costume supply store for a gangster-themed party Charbel had had for his housewarming. He'd gotten a little carried away—in fact, he'd bought two guns so that he could put one on each of his hips. The larger, heavier one was still there on the shelf untouched.

This was how it was; they were always on the edge of hysteria, he and his father, like two old ladies afraid of the dark. He knew that there was something missing here, some essential piece of information he was meant to get and didn't. But he also knew that's what made people, all those things you don't get about them. His dad was stuck in some kind of pain he couldn't get out of, and no one knew what the pain was, maybe not even he did. Francis kept thinking of him standing at the front door in his underwear, looking fragile and confused as the eggs flew through their door.

But at this moment Francis was trying to push it all away for a while. He was in Charbel's shower looking around for soap, but Charbel obviously didn't have any and Francis was wondering if he really smelled that bad.

He towelled himself off and put on the old shirt he would change out of just before they left Jesús' house for the bars. In the living room Charbel was already dressed and sitting on the couch with a beer in his hand, watching cartoons. 'We heading to Jesús' soon?'

'Nah.'

'Nah, what?'

'He's coming here. Can't go to his place anymore.'

'Why not?'

'Mami banned you.'

Charbel raised his eyebrows and said it in that voice he put on when he wanted to act like a shit, 'You're not allowed to play with him anymore because your dad's being a dick.'

Shit. Banned like he was a twelve-year-old or something. He'd loved Mami, ever since for ever. Jesús hadn't said anything to him and he hadn't thought about Jesús in all of this. He'd forgotten about Jesús' family—what had happened to his dad in Chile, why they came here, how this stuff might have made him feel.

And so, after he and Jesús and Charbel had gone out, after Francis had smoked the joint that he'd picked up from a guy he used to sit next to in Mrs. Ong's Year Seven maths class, after they'd all got angry with each other and made up again and said, 'I love you, bro,' like drunk guys do, as they stumbled down the street, after Charbel had helped him break into an apartment block his father was building down the road to steal a jackhammer, and they'd all dragged it down the street towards Francis' house and Francis had told him that he needed to do this by himself, after Francis had told Jesús 'you tell Mami to come by our house tomorrow morning'—after all that, he found himself alone in the front yard of his own home with a jackhammer.

Here he was again: three in the morning. On one side there was that half-finished apartment block looming over their house, on the other side, Lucy's house, old and familiar. His own home sat there solid and unmoveable, held in place between them. The street lights threw rectangular shapes across the concrete of his front yard. All the rules of daytime were gone. There was the smell of paint thinner on the brushes his dad had lined up to dry at the side of the house. That smell mixed with the herbs that grew in small pots hanging along the window frame. In his right hand the jackhammer was cold and heavy. He couldn't be bothered to lift it up all the way so it scraped across the concrete. It sounded like chalk against a chalkboard. He couldn't stand the sound. He watched a light flick on in his parents' house the moment he dropped it to the concrete.

Electricity. He needed electricity to get it going. He had forgotten about the simple details of things again. He remembered the plug at the side of the house near the bins. He could feel the concrete pulsating, already, underneath his feet as he plugged it in.

When he started the motor, the hammer jolted through his entire body. He held it in the same spot for what felt like a really long time. When the drill bit hit the ground beneath the concrete, the concrete cracked and he could knock it aside with his foot, like scooping out ice-cream with a spoon.

The lights in the house across the road came on. Windows opened up; faces appeared cautiously at first, then hung out shouting. He couldn't stop. The drilling held him captive. He was drilling his way out of there. Right to the other side of the earth.

Over the sound of his own drilling he could just make out the words 'fucking dickhead' being hurled at him from somewhere. His hands slipped and the jackhammer went skidding across the concrete. Its drill bit lodged itself in the house's aluminium siding and then stopped. There was silence for a moment before he heard the sirens coming. He began to run— out of habit more than anything else, really. He made it two blocks down the street before he turned to see his father standing there, wearing only his underwear, his arms crossed, red and blue lights casting shadows over him.

29

Clare arrived at Town Hall Station well before she was due at the movies, and a good thing she had started early because she'd been swallowed up by the force of the bodies shoved up against each other, taking up every bit of road and pavement so that the grey shades of the city could no longer be seen. It felt as though she had been lifted up against her will and put down somewhere unfamiliar. Up on the top of Town Hall steps a woman was shouting through a megaphone about small islands in the Pacific Ocean where the Australian government wanted to take all the refugees and lock them up in cages. It sounded like the plot of some dystopian novel and Clare wasn't sure that she quite believed it. Next to her, an elderly woman held up a poster of a child whose face looked too old for her body. She thrust the poster into the air and screamed *No!* every time the speaker on the steps said anything, as though she were speaking for the girl in her absence.

Then the crowd moved towards Hyde Park in a wave that took her with it. On one side there were the restless legs of horses, whose steel-capped hooves hit the ground with a thump that sounded like a gate being slammed shut over and over again. On the other side, the crowd screamed at the police on top of the horses. Clare stood still in the middle, closed her eyes against the people moving and pushing around her and the horses and their long legs. She felt the weight of it all, of everything, and it made her hands shake. When she opened her eyes slightly, there was a man on the ground with a bloody nose and two police officers pulling him along by his hand-cuffed hands. She wanted to shoot up into the sky and out of this. And then next to her, there he was, in that same 59Fifty hat. Maybe it was the same kid grown older, or maybe she was making it all up in her head. It looked like the kid she remembered from the last class she'd ever taught—the same dark shadows under his eyes, those freckles merging over the bridge of his nose, the jaw that looked like it was slightly caved in on one side. For a few minutes he had locked his arm through hers and pulled her somehow gently and forcefully at the same time towards the footpath, away from the moving stream of people. And then he had nodded slightly and left her there and she watched the crowd move forward, pulsating with all those things they wanted people to hear about the children who cut themselves in detention centres, and the men who ended their own lives by throwing their bodies onto the barbed-wire fences, and the women from those boats who washed up on the shores with their babies in their dead arms. There were thousands of them, screaming, crying, dancing, walking on their way towards Hyde Park.

When, finally, she had made it the two blocks down the street to the theatre, she wasn't sure how to tell Paul all the things she had seen, though he must have been part of it himself.

He was there in the entrance, leaning against a white wall, watching George Street, where the angry traffic was just starting to move again. Clare opened her mouth and made no noise. She pointed towards where the crowds had been and Paul nodded, 'Yeah, I was there for a while. Just listening.' Something felt like it had snapped between them, like a warmth that was there yesterday wasn't there today.

And then they were sitting in the dark, just she and Paul. And even though they were alone there was the smell of damp bodies from the night before, when it had rained and people must have sought shelter here. Clare wanted to sit, alone, in the dark and damp for the rest of the night, watching whatever came next until they asked her to leave. Her fingers kept brushing against Paul's as they reached into the giant bag of M&Ms that sat between them and waited for the previews to begin. She looked at him side-on; he looked older in this light, he had a sharper angle to his face that would have made him look dignified in a photograph.

'I met,' Clare began to say, 'I think I met that boy Ahmed, well he'd be a man now, actually, the kid who fell over in my class. The one with the hat.'

Paul turned and looked at her in the dim light.

'Yeah, I suppose that makes sense, all that time he spent in Villawood. He'd have something to protest.'

'Was he? I didn't realise.'

Paul looked at her, like he was searching her face for a reaction. 'That's why he had all those issues. He'd been locked up for so long. Everyone thought that you must have known . . . sometimes you just don't seem very capable of thinking about people all that hard.'

'I didn't—' Clare started to say and then looked at his lips, the steely purpleness of them in the reflection of the movie screen. She leant in further and kissed him there, gently, as though this one small act might excuse her for everything she had ever done.

Paul rolled a single small chocolate in his mouth and looked at the screen.

'It doesn't make up for anything, you know.'

He did, she was sure, know everything she was thinking.

She looked at him and thought about moving in again, of putting her hand high up on his leg. She didn't know, couldn't think of what else could be done, but as she began to move towards him he got up, slowly, *with grace*, her mother might say and walked down the aisle and towards the exit.

30

Upstairs, Antonio was in the bathtub. Downstairs, Rose was on the couch. Neither of them noticed that their spaces had begun to merge. Four hours ago, Antonio had turned the tap on and left it that way, falling asleep under the stream of water that flowed across his aching leg and out of the bathtub and through the cracks in the bathroom tiles, into the floor cavity and out through the light fittings in the living room where it was slowly trickling on the floor, not so far from where Rose stood at the window, not noticing.

Rose was looking out the window at the torn-up concrete of her front yard, imagining pulling back all that cracked concrete with a rake. She imagined she could take the front yard apart piece by piece by inserting the metal prongs underneath the cracks and pushing upwards. Antonio believed he'd been forced unfairly to the margins of something, and there were moments when, out of fear for him, she had silently agreed. He'd gone out to some wild place, so far from other human beings. She protected him, now, by not talking to him. Rose knew if she tried she would not be able to talk, she would scream.

And because the only way she did communicate with him now was in the look on her face, she made sure not to look at him this morning, after they'd both been up all night watching the concrete, waiting for what might happen next. She knew that if he looked at her he would know that she had crossed the line fully and completely now. Rose knew she was no longer who she had been; she was becoming a different person. Someone sharper, leaner, someone ready to leave for good.

Here was her front yard, here was her home, the one that Antonio had built for her. She thought about these things with a sense of detachment, as though they may not be a part of herself anymore. At one time it had seemed like the beginning of a whole new world, and it had been. Right now, more than forty years later, she was struck by how simple it all had been, how easy and satisfying to realise that a kind of security lay in a walk around her garden, a square brick house, the feeling of holding someone else's sweating palm. It had seemed to promise more. Now she thought, perhaps it didn't promise much at all.

Upstairs in the bathtub, Antonio was dreaming of St. Francis wandering in his beggar's robes through the odd combination of summits and high plateaux and low sunken plains of the mountains of Reggio Calabria. St. Francis was slim and hunched over, quick moving, always disappearing and reappearing somewhere else. He was there between the olive and bergamot trees in Antonio's family orchard, looking out across the Strait of Messina, leaning on his cane. He was watching for the sorceress Morgan le Fay who was using her witchcraft again to conjure up castles and boats out there, floating clear and hollow on the ocean. You never knew where they might be or what. Le Fay and her sirens were using their witchcraft to lure a hungry population out of their *pensiones* and into the ocean, to their death. But St. Francis was here to protect them. He emerged from behind one of the olive trees and stepped into the water, turned clear and shapeless and floated towards the mirage. When he emerged back on land he was whole and hard but cold as water. He touched the faces of those villagers looking out to the sea with his icy hands and said *no, don't leave, don't get on those boats*, but they smiled awkwardly and shook their heads.

In this dream he was back to the age of twenty-three, the year he left. The days were becoming weeks were becoming months and the wet was closing in again. He didn't know where his brother Christopher was but he'd left his new jacket on the hook behind the door. Antonio took it off the hook and put it on. The outside was heavy leather but on the inside it was lined with soft suede; the impractical garment of a farmer's son who did no farming. In the pocket Antonio found a wad of lira tied with a rubber band. He walked out to the balcony, a scrawny young man in a powerful coat and looked out to his father's orchard only a few metres away. Those bergamot trees his father had spent so long tending were bloated and over-grown. Their fruit, left unpicked while in season, had fallen to the ground and begun to rot in the wet. Their house was once there, behind the orchard, the houses of their neighbours were once there too before the last floods had sent them crashing down the mountain. Everyone had travelled north. Many got on boats and travelled even further than that, out across the seas.

He dreamt of rain. He dreamt he was back inside that apartment, packing a bag with the impractical objects of some-one who had nothing: a photo of his father, a statue of St. Francis, a tin of coffee. Antonio left his home in August 1961. It was the Calabrian in him. All those years of staring at water. He walked towards the main road where he would hitch a ride on the back of a truck, and then walk and then hitch and then take a train and then walk again, until he arrived at the Port of Naples where he would eventually board a boat. He did not look back except in that brief moment before he managed to flag down the truck. He looked back at those miraculous sand-stone houses on the main road, the ones that were still there, after all the bombs and all the floods, and remembered the beauty in those things that didn't wash away.

When he finally reached the Australian Immigration Office in the Port of Naples, Antonio was still practising the words he had learnt on his long journey there. His nervous energy had dissipated, leaving him scooped out, hollow. His hands sweated in his pockets. The foreign shape of those English words sat so awkwardly on his tongue. He held them in his mouth for a few moments, knowing that when he released them they would determine the shape of the rest of his life. These were the things that broke his heart as he stood there: the memory of his mother's small hands shelling peas, the steel grey of the sky before it rained, the knowledge of how hard it would be to become a new person in a new place, and the work he'd have to do to defend the person he would become. And now, he looked at this man at his desk, running his hand through his sandy-blond hair as though he was thinking really hard. A friend in the village had told him you needed to be two-thirds white to get into Australia but no one seemed to know what that meant. The words escaped his lips like a cough you can't hold back: 'I would like to get on a boat.'

Sometimes it was that earlier self that emerged. That straggly boy, wandering the same mountains as St. Francis, plotting his escape. Suddenly, he woke up in that bathtub. But he was still there in the other place with that voice that was never big enough to say *no* with any sense of conviction. He felt lonely and afraid. It was like being possessed by a lesser version of himself. At these times he could feel his former self pushing up against his skin from the inside, checking to see if it was safe to expose itself to the outside world, and then, just as suddenly, he was himself again. The adolescent despair sank down deep into his gut, near the base of his spine, and when he brought his hands up from the water and to his face he saw that they were shrivelled and worn. He was a man again, lying in the bathtub in the house that he had built so close to the mouth of the Parramatta River, where salt water met fresh and the boats could go no further.

It was one of those early evenings down by the river that was so heartbreakingly beautiful it made Antonio want to swallow the landscape. One of those nights where the sun melted into the water like butter in a frying pan, and the fog rolled in close to the ground so that it felt as though he was walking through sky. Since he had stopped thinking clearly, his body had been moving without him giving it instructions, as though it was doing the thinking his mind was too muddled to do. Today, his legs took him along the path next to the Parramatta River. He walked down one side and over the Lennox Bridge and then continued back down the river on the opposite bank. He had wanted, really, to be alone, to work out his thoughts, but Nico had just shown up again, so they walked together, talking of that new boatload of 237 Iraqis which had been picked up off the coast, the ones the television said had thrown their children into the sea.

The sound of Nico's voice was cut by the music coming from boomboxes playing Mandarin love songs. Chinese women old and young, they were on the Parramatta Ferry Pier again, stretching from right to left and then holding their arms out slowly with care. They stretched their arms out, they pulled them back. They did it again and again until a boat appeared further down the river between the mangroves, as if it had been hiding there waiting to be summoned. There was the tin sound of the music clocking over in rhythms that moved to a different beat than the ones he was used to, and then Nico was saying something about all those boat people having nothing to lose and the people smugglers who were the root of all evil and then Antonio was watching the boat come in and he was looking at the bodies crowded on its front deck. They were crammed up against the railing, taking pictures of themselves and the river, talking, laughing, carrying on like they didn't care that there were so many of them and such little room and they were about to get out, right here in his neighbourhood.

Nico put his hand between Antonio's shoulder blades and moved him gently forward until they were right there between the small portable bridge which had been thrown out to let the people off the boat and onto shore and where the Chinese women were holding their arms out wide and pulling them in again—beckoning everyone to come to shore. Antonio stood and watched the people coming off the boat. He could tell they'd come from many places, black people and yellow people and pale people with purple streaks of hair and then he was moving with the crowd that was boarding the boat. He hadn't wanted to go anywhere, but now he was here standing near the doorway with all the bodies pushing, pushing against him, and he didn't know where Nico had gone and he found himself alone in a crowd at the front of the boat where he could look through the open door and watch the captain on the bridge. Antonio watched him, this foreign-looking man with his dark, tight curly hair and his too-tanned skin. He watched him fiddling with all those dials and knobs like he was planning something, and Antonio thought of all the children on board, and all the children people had been throwing out into the sea, they were all there waiting, and he could see through the captain's window that it had begun to rain heavily, and he knew that soon those paths by the river would become submerged in water and they'd all be stranded out here so close to land and so far away, and no one would come to their rescue.

He touched the gun in his coat pocket and moved through

the door until he was standing two feet behind the captain, who hadn't noticed him yet. Antonio watched the captain from behind, the way he carried his body and he was thinking that something there reminded him of his brother whom he had walked out on all those years ago, and then right at that moment Nico appeared standing next to him in that tinny box of a room and Nico said, 'You know life doesn't really bring you into the future, it just throws you further and further into the past.'

And Antonio nodded and said, 'I know. It's something I'm just now beginning to understand.'

And it was that conversation that made the captain turn around suddenly to see who was behind him, and it was then that Antonio pulled out the gun and placed it firmly between the captain's eyes.

Antonio at that moment had a serene look on his face, that's what the security cameras showed later on, and that's what puzzled people so much, even the captain, at that moment, about why this man was here and what he was trying to achieve. It was this image that would appear in all the newspapers the following day: the one with Antonio, his lips slightly open, the gun held firmly at the captain's forehead. Curiously, in that image he didn't appear to actually be looking at the captain at all but at the empty piece of air beside him, as if he was caught mid-conversation with someone who wasn't there. One of the headlines read: 'No More Boats', with the subheading, 'From Tampa to Parramatta, Australians want the boats turned around'. The pull-out quote was the words of John Howard, the ones Antonio had been thinking about so much of late: *We will decide who comes to this country and the circumstances in which they come.* For the roughly twelve hours between early morning when people got their papers and late evening when every TV station interrupted what they were playing to show the footage of the planes crashing into the twin towers, the picture was everywhere. Before all the news stories that made us draw all those connections between Muslims in planes and Muslims in boats, there was Antonio Martone, the Italian immigrant who was trying to stop all those ferries coming up the Parramatta River with his plastic gun.

NOTES ON SOURCES

The creation of this fictional work has involved spending time with a lot of fascinating books, people, archival material, websites, magazines, and a lot of time walking around my neighbourhood. My research has taken me off in directions too numerous to account for, but I would like to acknowledge some of the sources that have helped form the bulk of ideas I have explored creatively here. I would particularly like to pay my respects to some of the brave, challenging and in-depth research being done in the area of Australian cultural studies and asylum seeker policy.

For my research into Tampa I have primarily referred to *Dark Victory*, by David Marr and Marian Wilkinson (Allen and Unwin, 2004), as well as Frank Brennan's *Tampering with Asylum: A Universal Humanitarian Problem* (UQP, 2003). The latter is where I found Solicitor General David Bennett's quote, which has also been widely cited elsewhere.

Fiona Allon's *Renovation Nation: Our Obsession with Home* (UNSW Press, 2008) helped to shape much of my novel's discussion about building, McMansions and the meaning of home in the era of John Howard. The notes that the anti-McMansion protesters leave around the estate Francis and Antonio work on are adapted from similar notes quoted in Allon's book.

I have read and reread both of Anthony Burke's landmark texts, *Beyond Security, Ethics and Violence: War Against the Other* (Routledge, 2007), and *Fear of Security: Australia's*

Invasion Anxiety (Cambridge University Press, 2008), both of which have shaped many of the overarching themes about anxiety in this work.

Lastly, I'd like to acknowledge Azadeh Dastyari, whose work I've been following over twenty years of friendship, conversation and questioning, and whom I never fail to admire for her incredible humanity and unwavering commitment to the important job of researching and publishing work on asylum seekers.

ACKNOWLEDGEMENTS

I would like to sincerely thank the staff and students at the Writing and Society Research Centre at Western Sydney University for their support in writing this book. I would particularly like to thank Gail Jones and Ivor Indyk who both supervised my PhD thesis, where much of the research and writing of this book was undertaken. Ivor, thank you in addition for taking this book all the way through to its publication and for continuing to teach me so much about writing. I would also like to acknowledge the continued support that I have received from Parramatta Council. Undertaking a residency at the Parramatta Artists Studios for two years during the writing of this book has provided me with both the physical and mental space I needed to finish it as well as the privilege of working alongside so many inspiring artists. I would particularly like to thank the coordinator, Sophia Kouyoumdjian, for her unwavering support and commitment to both myself and the arts in my community.

Thank you to my husband, Michael, for always encouraging my writing and to our son, Zain, who would prefer I play with him. Thank you to my parents and to my brother for their support over a lifetime.

About the Author

Felicity Castagna was awarded the Prime Minister's Literary Award in 2014 for her previous novel, *The Incredible Here and Now*, which was adapted for the stage by the National Theatre of Parramatta. Her collection of short stories, *Small Indiscretions*, was named an *Australian Book Review Book* of the Year. Her work has also appeared on national radio and television. *No More Boats* was a finalist both for the Miles Franklin Literary Award and the Voss Literary Prize. Castagna lives in Sydney.